STAR CHAMBER

ISBN: 978-0-9988777-7-8 (hardback)
        978-0-9988777-8-5 (paperback)
        978-0-9988777-9-2 (ebook)

STAR CHAMBER

A Jeannie Loomis Novel

GARY J. ROSE

ALSO BY GARY J. ROSE

Towards the Integration of Police Psychology
Techniques to Combat Juvenile Delinquency in
K-12 Schools

Hitting Rock Bottom

Teaching Inside the Walls

How to Create a Public-School Military Style Boot-
Camp Academy

Ark of the Covenant – Raid on the Church of Our
Lady Mary of Zion
(A Jeannie Loomis Novel)

For Mike Lake and his canine companion Ripley

Mom

My daughter Mandy

PROLOGUE

The Star Chamber was an English court that met in the Royal Palace of Westminster from the late 15th century to the mid-17th century. It was created to supplement the judicial activities of common-law and equity courts in civil and criminal matters. Its goal was to curtail socially and politically prominent people, who were so powerful that ordinary courts hesitated to convict them of their crimes, allowing them to be "beyond the law."

The Star Chamber's procedures gave it considerable advantages over ordinary courts. It was less bound by rigid form; it did not depend upon juries either for indictments or a verdict, it could act upon the petition of an individual complaint or upon information received, and it could place an accused person under oath to answer a petitioner's bill and reply to detailed questioning. (www.britannica.com/topic/Star-Chamber)

The judicial activity of Star Chamber grew with greatest rapidity during the chancellorship of Thomas

Wolsey (1515). In addition to prosecuting rioters and other committing such crimes, Wolsey used the court with increased vigor against perjury, slander, forgery, fraud, offenses against legislation and the king's proclamations, and any action considered a breach of the peace.

Cases began upon petition or information and depositions were taken from witnesses in the absence of a jury. Those that supported law and order believed that the Star Chamber was very effective.

*In the 21st century, a clandestine
Star Chamber was re-established due to civil unrest
that seemed to spring up throughout the United States
on a weekly basis. It was modeled similarly to its
predecessor, but this time it targeted those who aimed
at destroying the United States.*

CHAPTER 1

J eannie Loomis arrived at the Interpol office to see Agent Delaney at the agreed upon time. She was greeted by the receptionist. "Good morning Agent Loomis. Agent Delaney is expecting you. Please go in." The receptionist was the one who greeted her and her team several weeks earlier in what became a career stopper for her: the investigation of Frank Silva, Dr. Nancy Bell, and the former infamous rogue former military unit, the Banshees. After months of surveillance and planning, it appeared to Jeannie Loomis, that Frank and the Banshees, as well as Dr. Bell, were ready to attempt the theft of the presumably existent Ark of the Covenant from a small chapel located in Axom, Ethiopia.

The end result of her investigation was that suspects in the case were lost: Frank Silva, Dr. Bell and all members of the Banshees. The first ground crew that arrived in Axom, found no trace of any of the culprits, no evidence that the small chapel had been breached, nor that any theft had taken place. It was as if the suspects had simply vanished.

"Hello, Agent Loomis," said Agent Delaney with his British accent, as he stood upon Loomis' entrance to his office. "Please have a seat," while motioning to a chair across from his desk. "How have you been under the circumstances?"

"Please, call me Jeannie," she replied as she continued: "Well, let's see. As has been pointed out several times by my superiors, I have spent Bureau money, time, and resources trying to catch Frank Silva, Dr. Bell, and the Banshees for their involvement in the international theft of the "mythical" Ark of the Covenant. In the end, not only can I not locate any of the suspects, but I also lost one of the Banshees, who was an informant working with the AFT on weapon smuggling out of Afghanistan. So, to answer your question, I'm fucked. Pardon my French."

"I completely understand the frustration you feel," Delaney said. I also took some flack regarding this investigation, but I am afraid you took the brunt of it. By the way, would you like some coffee?" He picked up the phone to place a request with his receptionist, but Loomis declined his offer. He returned the phone to its base and continued. "I wish I could provide you with more information, but we still have no leads regarding any of the subjects involved. We explored the last known position of the yacht but found no wreckage or human remains. It too seems to have vanished. As you are aware, we had negative results reported by our ground crew in Axom. There has been no chatter between any of the suspects, no social media action, no credit card usage, no bank transactions. If any of them are alive, I don't know how they are surviving."

Loomis just stared at Delaney, saying nothing and then stood thanking him for all of his agency's prior help and follow up reports and, after exchanging handshakes, left his office. She looked at her reflection in the windows of the Interpol building façade and could see the effects of stress on her body, especially her face.

She saw an average-build, washed-up, FBI agent, whose blond hair was due for a visit to a hairdresser. She was approaching a birthday that would put her south of forty-five. Married and divorced twice with no children, she realized that the Bureau was all she had left, and her career advancement had taken a huge hit due to the Ark investigation. She joined the agency right after college at the age of twenty-two and quickly advanced to supervisory ranks resulting in her transfer to several field offices each time. This, she told herself, created stress in her marriages, which resulted in her divorces. At least, that is how she justified her failed marriages. She never wanted children and in one of her marriages, the decision to not start a family added to the eventual destruction of their relationship. She smoked too much and had spiraled into a deep crevice of drinking heavily at times and waking with a sex partner she picked up at a bar. Fortunately, none of these escapades resulted in violent encounters, nor had she picked up any STDs. Now with her career on the rocks, she told herself that she was on the verge of losing whatever control she still had of her high-risk behavior.

She knew before going into the meeting with Delaney, that she would probably not glean any new information. But, since she already had her travel documents to Ethiopia in hand, she wanted to make sure that if he did have new information, she could follow-up on it when she arrived outside the chapel fencing.

CHAPTER 2

The doorman opened the door as the jogger approached. "Good morning, sir," he said, fully expecting a generous tip. He was not disappointed when he received a ten-dollar bill. The jogger did not say anything but quickly walked into the lobby of the high-rise. He walked to his mailbox and inserted his key. Inside he found a small package with no return address as well as a lot of junk mail which he quickly deposited into a strategically placed wastepaper basket by the mailboxes. He placed the package under his arm and proceeded to the bank of elevators to his right. The female front desk clerk smiled in a flirtatious manner, and he returned the smile. Might have to check her out later he thought.

Standing at 6"2" with dark brown hair and a chiseled face reflecting a lot of time at a gym, he made sure his walk was noticed by the desk clerk. Of course, wearing his tailored jogging suit helped show off his athletic build.

He entered the elevator but did not examine the package any further. He knew its contents. His apartment was spacious with over 2,000 square feet of living space more than a single male needed, but, due to its location in San Francisco, overlooking the bay, he was paying for the privilege of living in one of the most expensive locations in the city. After showering and a close shave, he dressed in a freshly pressed pair of slacks and a black pullover Massimo Alba sweater. Instead of socks, he chose slippers for the time being and sat at his desk grabbing the package and his collectible mail opener.

He shook the contents out onto his desk and saw what he was expecting: a small thumb drive. Before inserting the thumb drive into his Mac, he walked about the room making sure all the window coverings were in place. He then secured his earplugs and inserted the drive. He smiled before anything appeared on his screen, thinking that this felt like the beginning of so many Mission Impossible films. He started humming the theme song of the many MIP films. "I can't remember how many films have been made," he thought. "He does perform the destruction of the drive after review, so maybe drawing the comparison is not too far-fetched."

He instantly recognized the face of the former Secretary of State, Virginia McKenzie, whose face filled the screen. "Bitch," he said to himself out loud. Several slides showed her residence and her most recent daily activities. The next slide showed an empty courtroom in the background and a short heading: Guilty - Level One Sentence.

He removed the thumb drive and walked into the bathroom. There he removed a plastic bottle with a liquid substance from under the basin and put on rubber gloves that covered his hands and arms up to his elbows. As he turned on the light he heard the overhead fan activate so he knew there was plenty of ventilation in the bathroom before performing the task at hand. He placed the thumb drive in a glass jar and then, slowly poured the liquid from the plastic bottle into the jar. The thumb drive hissed and quickly dissolved into nothing. He then opened the lid to his toilet and flushed the liquid. Securing the lid on the larger plastic bottle he placed it back under the basin and then removed his plastic protective gloves and placed them in a larger plastic bag which he rolled up and put alongside the plastic bottle. All of the documents he copied from the thumb drive had been shredded after being thoroughly reviewed.

He entered his kitchen and poured himself a glass of Grey Goose and dropping in three olives skewered on a toothpick. A small dash of Vermouth, and he was ready to consider his plan for the assassination.

CHAPTER 3

The plane arrived in Ethiopia thirty-seven minutes late, but Jeannie was in no hurry. She was not prepared for the heat that hit her in her face while walking out of the airport. Finding a waiting taxi, she asked the driver to take her to Axom. What she hoped to find she did not know. She convinced herself that this trip was necessary if just to bring closure to the whole disastrous investigation. What had happened to Frank, Dr. Bell, and their former military conspirators? How could they completely disappear? What about their equipment? And the boat? How does a mega-yacht with several people aboard vanish into thin air? Does the guardian have any information?

She checked into the same hotel used by Frank and Nancy. The female desk clerk was not on duty until the next morning and the male co-worker was no help at all. He had no idea who Dr. Nancy Bell or Frank were since he had only recently been hired by the hotel. She decided to take a cold shower and then when the sun started its descent to the west she would explore the grounds around the chapel.

Jeannie kicked off her shoes, stripped off her sweat-drenched blouse and bra, then removed her dark pants and underwear. She stood briefly in front of the rectangular mirror hanging on the inside door of the bathroom door. Jeannie was 5'6" with long blond hair normally wore in a ponytail for work. Most people that saw her would describe her as very pretty with an hourglass figure. After examining her body for a few seconds, she came to the same conclusion: she still looked pretty good for her age, but believed that she spotted some new stress lines on her forehead. The damned bullshit the bureau put her through with the Ark investigation caused them she thought.

After drying off except for allowing her hair to air dry, she put on a pair of shorts and a sports bra. She felt much better with her wet hair. She walked to a window that overlooked Axom, specifically the chapel. There it stood: just as it appeared, exactly in the center of all the pictures she and her team displayed in their "war room" during the Ark investigation.

Looking at it from across the street, the chapel did not distinguish itself differently than some of the missions established by Junipero Sierra in California between 1769 and 1833 that Jeannie had visited with her parents in her youth. She recognized it was built in neo-Byzantine style from a few art classes taken in college; it was almost a square tan colored box.

There was a round dome on the roof but, since it is so small, it looked misplaced. It had only one door for both entrance and exit, and the whole chapel was surrounded by a small, maybe five-foot tall wrought iron fence.

She thought of the effort Frank and his conspirators had taken to help financed his plan to create the chapel replica in the Arizona desert, and how exacting Frank's recreated chapel specs were as she viewed the actual structure. She never learned how Frank, Nancy and the Banshees were going to execute the theft, but with their expertise, she did not feel the chapel would offer too much resistance. But, she thought, what were they going to do with the guardian? She heard stories that he was a fragile elderly man, so physically he would be easy prey for the Banshees to overcome - but how? How could they have assaulted this building located almost in the center of town? Were there other security measures that she was not aware of, that somehow Frank and Nancy had acquired? Oh, maybe she would get some answers in the morning, but it was now time to get some dinner and call it a night.

Eight-thousand, six-hundred and forty-two miles away from his target, the assassin mapped out his plan to eliminate of one the most liberal of former Secretaries of State, while drinking his third vodka martini.

CHAPTER 4

The Star Chamber was in session twenty-four hours earlier. The judges arrived in their vehicles separately at a predetermined time. Punctuality was absolute. No Uber or taxis were allowed. Only those in attendance knew of its location and the secrecy surrounding it.

The court was located in what Europeans would call a villa: A three story massive structure with over seventy-five rooms. The landscape surrounding the building was immaculate with a manicured lawn, topiary, and several fountains. Inside, there was a large ballroom located to the rear of the building that had been converted into a mock courtroom. Eleven high-back red leather chairs were placed behind a solid cherry wood semi-circle table with a large area across from them where a huge television was hanging. Two computers were sitting on a much lower computer stand to the side of the television. The room was sound proof, and per standard operation procedures, the Sergeant of Arms had scanned the room for any electronic surveillance devices.

The first person to enter the chamber was Judge Wayne Katamoto, a retired superior court judge. He, like the other entering judges, wore a traditional black robe. He was soon joined by eight other judges. Small conversations took place among the judges as they took their seats waiting for the anticipated striking of the gavel on the walnut block by Judge Katamoto. As silence engulfed the chamber, Katamoto called the judges to order and looking at a single piece of paper laying in front of him, said, "Our case tonight is that of former Secretary of State Virginia McKenzie." He then picked up a wireless presenter, aimed it at the television an a picture of the former Secretary of State appeared on the screen. Judge Katamoto heard some stirring coming from some of those in attendance, and interpreted the murmuring as unflattering comments. He paused, and those whispering got the hint and became quiet.

"Secretary McKenzie is accused of high treason" he stated while advancing to the next slide.

While in office she violated the sacred trust placed in her by the citizens of the United States.

I will now outline the various charges against the defendant. Upon concluding, he asked if any of the judges had a question or comment. The only comment came from Judge Silverman who wanted an additional charge filed against the former secretary.

His charge easily fell within the treason classification agreed upon by the Star Chamber.

Judge Kanamoto queried the other judges and with a unanimous vote, the additional charge was added. He then picked up a laminated card and read the following:

"The defendant, Virginia McKenzie, has been charged with treason against the United States. Only upon a unanimous verdict by this court, will sentencing be pronounced. At this time, I will call the roll for your verdict."

"Judge Roberts?"

"Guilty."

"Judge Swartz?"

"Guilty."

"Judge Baldwin?"

"Guilty."

"Judge Kalford?"

"Guilty."

"Judge Hall?"

"Guilty."

"Judge Silverman?"

"Guilty."

"Judge Henderson?"

"Guilty."

"Judge Kavanaugh?"

"Guilty."

"At this time, I will enter my judgment which is guilty. We have a unanimous verdict of a Guilt -Level

One Sentence. I make the motion to notify the SDL for immediate execution of our verdict. All in favor say aye."
"Aye."

CHAPTER 5

T he assassin chose the 4th of July, not for the irony of what was going to take place on this historic day, but in hopes that some individuals would continue to set-off fireworks in the early morning hours which he would use as a distraction. The trip to Delaware was uneventful other than setting up a date with someone he considered the most attractive flight attendant on board the early morning flight. "Why is it that most males fantasize about making love to a flight attendant? Must be the uniform," he thought.

Hailing an Uber, he instructed the driver to take him to the Hotel Du Pont. He refrained from engaging in any real conversation with the driver but did give him a nice tip upon completion of the trip. Since no one would be able to connect him to the "hit," he was not concerned about his brief interaction with the driver.

Hotel Du Pont was to his liking: - a five-star hotel located in Wilmington in a downtown 1913 landmark sitting across the street from Rodney Square, and was

6 miles from Winterthur Museum, which he needed to visit at three o'clock that afternoon. He checked in at the front desk where a very handsome African-American male greeted him when he approached.

"Good afternoon sir. May I help you?"

"Yes," the assassin said, "I have a reservation." He then handed the clerk his American Express card while inquiring about the hours of the museum. The clerk produced a pamphlet showing the museum, pictures of a few exhibits and the posted hours. He figured he could easily grab a quick lunch there in the hotel and then take a leisurely walk to the institution.

He refused help with his luggage and approached the banks of elevators. Entering one, he punched number eight for his floor. He found his room and entered. After placing his luggage on the bed, he took off his jacket, placed it in the closet and then checked out each room - pulling the drapes closed in two of them. He turned on the air condition finding the suite too warm for his liking. The suite was much smaller than his digs in San Francisco, but nicely laid out he thought. He first removed his clothing and placed them in two of the drawers of what he believed was a Campania Mirrored Armoire.

He plugged in his cellphone to charge, but still used it to call the flight attendant and confirm their date for later that evening. She answered on the third ring and together they decided to meet at The Green Room, a high-end French cuisine and wine dining place where diners are served in a formal dining room of a 1913 Italian Renaissance hotel. Again, he was not overly concerned about having a brief interaction with the flight attendant since nothing would be traced back to him after he completed his assignment.

He ordered room service and had a light lunch. He opted for an ice tea versus a cocktail, figuring he would make up for that on his date. It was a little brisk outside when he left the hotel lobby heading to the museum. He pulled the collar of his camel hair jacket over his neck and shoved his hands in its pockets. It did not take long to reach the museum.

Avoiding the many exhibits being advertised upon entering the museum, he headed to one of the many gardens surrounding the building. He held on to the brochure given to him earlier by the hotel desk. Spotting the contact he was looking for, approached a middle-aged female wearing a hat, faux fur coat and an extremely large purse. She did not glance at him at first, fixating on a fountain with a waterwheel. Then, as if on cue, she made a statement on how the sound of splashing water had a calming effect.

He responded by saying that he once visited Niagara Falls in a boat and the sound of the crashing water did not make him feel calm. She smiled and after looking around, reached into her purse and pulled out a large bag. After handing it to him, she said, "good luck," turned, and left him standing there alone.

Before leaving the museum, he faked his interest in a few exhibits and then purchased a large black coffee for his return trip to the Du Pont. The bag was moderately heavy as he expected and was amazed at how easily his contact removed and handed the property to him. He sipped his coffee as he walked thinking not only about his hot date, but also the plan he had devised. He knew that no plan was full proof; but, he was a firm believer that, like many professional athletes who can envision an intended goal, it helps one complete a task - or something like that.

CHAPTER 6

J eannie awakened to sunlight entering through the windows and the consequential warming of the room. She could not recall the lousy nightmare she had but knew that the sweat dampening her t-shirt was not due to the room temperature. More likely, she thought, it had to do with the whole Ark affair and the damn bureau.

And then a random thought entered her head. When did she have her last period? A slight panic attack caused her breathing to increase a little. She started backtracking in her mind when she had her last period, and when she had her last sexual playtime. "Shit," she thought, "…no time to spend on this right now. I need to see if the female clerk is at the front desk and then grab breakfast. If I'm really lucky, I might catch the guardian outside the chapel and find out what happened to Frank and his gang."

She opted for a lightweight pair of pants and blouse and walking shoes. She tied her hair into a ponytail and went down to the desk. Much to her delight, there was a female clerk on duty.

"Hello," Jeannie said.

"Hello, how did you sleep?" the clerk asked

"Well, thank you," Jeannie replied. "I'm wondering if you could help me." She pulled two pictures from her back pocket: one of Dr. Nancy Bell and the other of Frank Silva. She laid them on the top of the desk facing the clerk.

"Have you ever seen these individuals?" she asked.

With a smile on her face, the clerk instantly said, "Yes, this is Dr. Nancy and her boyfriend. I cannot remember his name but they were both here at least two times." Without taking a breath she continued, "The strangest thing however, one day they were here and then they just disappeared. They did not pay their bill and when we checked their room, even their luggage was gone. It was as if they were never here." She continued to look at the two pictures.

Jeannie slowly picked up the two pictures and said she was concerned about their welfare and began asking further questions. After approximately five minutes of questions and answers, Jennie knew very little more than before. Yes, Nancy Bell and Frank Silva stayed at this hotel on two occasions. The clerk related that Bell told her she was a professor and conducting research on the chapel and the Ark of the Covenant. She said that Frank was generally quiet but Nancy loved to talk. She had hoped that Dr. Nancy, who took pictures of her, might put them in a book someday. Sadly, she said, she went home after her normal shift and the last time she saw Dr. Nancy was when she and her boyfriend went out to dinner.

Jeannie never felt the necessity of identifying herself to the clerk, nor the reason for being there in Ethiopia. After all, technically she was on vacation--not on bureau business. She thanked the clerk, and after getting directions to a restaurant serving breakfast, she began what she hoped would be a more productive day.

After breakfast, Jennie walked towards the chapel. There were already over a hundred people there to pay homage to the building, mostly females with children. One woman who was carrying what appeared to be a bag of groceries walked to the front gate, place the bag at its foot, and then rang a bell mounted to a post near the fence

"Great," Jeannie thought, "If I'm fortunate, I can interview the guardian." She walked close to the gate and waited. After ten minutes she was about to give up and started walking back towards the hotel when she heard a door open and someone shuffling their feet. She looked at the entrance to the chapel and there he was. The guardian. He was a frail elderly man dressed in an olive-colored robe and sandals. He looked like he might be in his late sixties or early seventies. He initially focused on the bag of groceries and started to walk towards it. Then he stopped and gazed directly at Jeannie. His eyes were deeply seated.

He diverted his walk towards the bag of groceries and walked directly to the fence where Jeannie was standing. Initially speechless, Jeannie finally found her voice and said, "Hello." The guardian did not reply; he simply stared at her. Not knowing what else to say, she pulled out the two pictures of Dr. Bell and Silva and held them near the fence at the guardian's eye level. She asked him if he had ever seen them? Again, no response.

While holding his eyes on Jeannie, he reached into a pocket of his robe with his left hand and pulled out a shiny necklace. His hands were very small, and he easily passed his hand with the object through the wrought iron fencing and handed it to Jeannie. He then retracted his hand, nodded to her, picked up the bag of groceries, and re-entered the chapel--not to be seen again by Jeannie.

She looked at the necklace and saw that it was a St. Christopher medal. Being Catholic, although non-practicing, she knew St. Christopher was the patron saint of travel. She wondered if this was something the guardian gave people who traveled to view the chapel. She will never learn that it was the medal held by Frank Silva the last day of his life.

CHAPTER 7

Arriving back at his suite after a non-eventful dinner date with the flight attendant, he removed the material given to him by the female courier from between the two bed mattresses where he had hidden it, and laid it out on the bedspread. It included a Sig Sauer P 226 9-millimeter with a loaded clip, one-hundred feet of Zipline and a Zipline gun, a pair of gloves, a Zipline harness, military-grade night googles, and finally--a bottle of Chloroform. He looked at the liquid and realized he had a smile on his face, recalling all those movies he had seen where the bad guy takes out a rag, douses it with Chloroform, and waits in the dark for the intended victim. Several minutes later as the music from the film indicates suspense, the victim appears and passes close to the suspect who immediately places the rag on the victim's nose, and if a few seconds the victim is unconscious.

"Doesn't work that way people," he thought. "First, if you pour the Chloroform onto a rag too early, it would evaporate losing most of its knockout capability. Secondly, even if you got the dose correctly, it would take an average size person about five-minutes of inhaling to bring the desired results. If the dose is too small, the 'victim' may get a headache. Too much and the victim could die."

No, in this case, he knew the victim's age, weight, and medical problems. He would have the exact dosage ready. All he needed was to make her feel lethargic and disoriented. Then, after she passed out, he could remove the liquid and arrange for the accident. Could it be found at autopsy? Sure, if the coroner decides to conduct a drug screen, but what the hell did he care? He would already be preparing for his next job.

Secretary McKenzie was seventy-years old, and although her gatekeepers tried to suggest she was in excellent health and a youthful seventy, those with medical knowledge could detect she had some Dysphasia, a brain condition that impairs speech-- even from watching her on television.

Also, a paparazzi got a shot of the former secretary's open purse and captured a picture of prescription pill bottles for Digoxin and some type of Diuretic. The former secretary had a bad heart. She was, by life insurance BMI standards, obese for her size, and this compounded her heart condition. Yet, the liberal former secretary yearned to be President of the United States, a position that she, with the support of her late husband, had wanted so badly before he passed away. She wanted the position, not so much for the

26

Executive branch, but for all the money that could be made before and after she held office.

It would be the 4th of July in a week and a half. While many Americans would be celebrating the holiday with hot dogs, watermelon, corn-on-the-cob, beer, soda, and backyard BBQs, the assassin would be preparing for the death of the former secretary of state.

CHAPTER 8

J eannie arrived back at the Dulles International Airport at 10:15 PM. Tired, disappointed and not looking forward to going back to the bureau tomorrow morning, she decided to stop at the airport bar and have a quick one. She ordered a Manhattan and told herself that she would only have one. She ran everything she learned from her trip to Ethiopia and still came up with nothing. Somehow, she had to let the Ark investigation go. But, how could everyone listed as suspects in this case just disappear? She tried to process what she knew.

Dr. Nancy Bell, a well-known academic and highly praised researcher, quit her job as a professor. Well, she didn't quit. She just never showed up when she was due to return. Had she and Frank Silva decided to screw the rest of the Banshees after finding something valuable, and split--not giving Frank's former black-up team their share? Or, could the Banshees have gotten wind that Bell and Silva were going to fuck them over, and in turn, take them out?

Judging from her visit to the chapel, it did not seem likely that the mission or chapel, or whatever, was ever breached. Physically everything seemed to be in place. Had they physically assaulted the building, there would not have been enough time to make repairs before her visit to the site.

The yacht was the easiest to dismiss. It simply could have sunk with everyone onboard. Sure, there were never any wreckage or any bodies found, but sharks could have taken care of that, right?

Oh well, she thought, someday it may become a great adventure/thriller novel—or hey, even a great movie. What was the name of that film with Harrison Ford, something about an Ark and Nazis?

She woke up sensing someone moving next to her in bed. Where in the hell was she? This was not her home. She slowly rolled over grabbing the top sheet to cover her nudity. He was lying on his back sound asleep. Not bad looking, but she had been with more handsome men.

Damn, why does she keep doing this? Does she have a death wish, or what?

She slowly climbed out of bed trying not to disturb whoever he was. She accomplished that as well as locating her clothes scattered throughout the motel room. She had to pee but did not want to run the risk of flushing the toilet and waking him up, so she decided to hold it and just get home. She could feel dampness between her legs and thoughts of missed periods re-entered her mind. What's wrong with me, she asked herself?

She arrived home and quickly headed to the bathroom. After relieving herself, she took the hottest shower she could stand. After glancing at the alarm clock next to her bed, she saw that she would arrive at work a few minutes late, but nothing that should get her into trouble--again. Dressed in a gray business suit and sliding her Glock 19 into her holster, she headed out the door. Another day--another dollar, she thought.

Jeannie arrived at the Roseville, California satellite office of the FBI. She preferred being stationed here versus working at the San Francisco office. She parked her Lexus in the secured employee parking lot. It was going to be a gorgeous day, she thought. There were a few fluffy clouds in the sky and just enough wind to unfold the flag in front of the federal building. After exchanging a few hellos to agents in the parking lot, she entered the building. Passing through security, she arrived at her office. Taped to her door was a note requesting that she see the SAC (Special Agent in Charge) as soon as possible. Shit, she thought, now what? She placed her purse and handgun in one of the desk drawers, locked it, grabbed a notepad and headed to the SAC's office.

She said, "Hi" to Stephanie, Davenport's poor secretary, who exchanged the greeting. Stephanie got up and knocked on the SAC's door. Without waiting for a response, she went in and was overheard telling Davenport that Jeannie was here to see him.

Jeannie entered and saw him sitting at his desk. With over thirty-years of experience in law enforcement, but only three in the bureau, Davenport was counting the days down to retirement. Unknown to him, his agents were also counting, wondering why the days were taking so long to pass. He was another Obama appointee. A typical brown-nose Democrat whose liberal ideologies had corrupted the bureau from the inside. It hurt the agents on the street doing their job, risking their lives, while political appointees like Davenport were doing everything they could to hinder any policy to be implemented by the new governing body.

"Loomis, have a seat," Davenport said.

She complied and waited for what was sure to be another ass-chewing. She could just feel it. But shit, she had been out of the country, so how could she be accused of fucking up something? Thoughts raced through her mind. No, the Ark investigation was the only thing that came up negative.

SAC Davenport thought that he could intimidate individuals by simply staring at them without further conversation until the person got so uncomfortable they felt compelled to start a dialogue. This ploy was now being used on Jeannie. Forcing against the urge to speak, she outlasted Davenport who gave in and started the conversation.

"What you do on your own time is none of the bureau's nor my concern as long as it's not criminal or brings shame to the department." He paused to see if she would say anything that he could use to cover his bruised ego since she did not become intimidated with his little interrogation techniques. Again, Jeannie remained silent.

Actually, by the time he said, "What you do on your own time…" she blushed, thinking that somehow he had learned of her little transgression the night before at the bar and the sex thing at the motel. God, how embarrassing. She was going to get a lecture on morals from her boss.

"Loomis, I understand that you recently returned from a trip to Ethiopia. Is that correct?" SAC Davenport asked.

My God, Jeannie thought, I am going to get raked over the coals again because of this God damn Ark investigation.

"Yes, sir. I returned last night," she replied.

He paused and just stared at her.

Starting to feel intimidated and not wanting him to feel proud of himself, she adjusted herself in the chair and said, "Is there a problem here?"

That seemed to throw Davenport off a little, shown by him having to clear his throat and move his eyes briefly away from Jeannie. "What was your purpose for going to Ethiopia, if I don't already know?" he asked.

"Yes sir, I believe you do already know, and with that in mind I don't see how it's a concern to the bureau." She wanted her statement to be pointed towards him and put him on the defensive, but thought better of it.

She continued, "I paid my expenses. I never identified myself as being with the FBI. I look at the trip as a long overdue vacation."

Davenport sneered at her and said, "A long-overdue vacation to a third world country? I could think of several other places I would want to visit on vacation (holding his hands up making quote signs) than Ethiopia." Not waiting for a reply, he said, "Loomis, I know the last several months before, and now after the Ark investigation, have been rough on you."

No shit, she thought; and it's because of bureaucratic assholes like you that my world seems to be spinning out of control. Jeannie continued to look at Davenport hopefully, without any body language showing how pissed-off she was.

Using a technique her training officer taught her years ago, she repeated word for word in her mind everything Davenport was saying, forcing herself to not make spontaneous responses. This gave her time to evaluate the ramifications of her speech and also gave the appearance that she cared about what he was saying.

She hated Davenport and many of the top brass of the new FBI that Obama had appointed during his term in office. They were liberal paper pushers who were more caught up in kissing the butt of the next level of administration over them for promotion purposes, than allowing the street agents to do their job. They were all caught up in the political correctness movement which was having a terrible effect on the morale of not only the FBI but all federal and local law enforcement agencies across the United States.

One of the big jokes in the bureau was that when Davenport finally retired from the bureau, his political leanings would make him a shoo-in candidate for governorship in California, quickly becoming the most liberal, yet laughing stock, of America. That state wants to make all bathrooms in the state gender-neutral. I bet any informed pervert loves that idea.

Even with these random thoughts going through her mind, she could still focus on the narrative coming from Davenport.

"Look," he said. "You're not in violation of any department regulations regarding your trip to Ethiopia. I just feel your decision-making abilities are in question, and felt that I needed to have a one-on-one with you, if not for your sake, for the sake of your team. I have always had an open-door policy, and in the future I hope you seek me out when something is bothering you." He stopped and waited for Jeannie's response.

Jeannie was sure that this asshole wanted to her say something like, "Oh, thank you so much. I feel much better knowing that you are in my corner and that I can come to you at any time." Fat chance of that happening.

Instead, she stood and looking at Davenport, saying, "You don't have to worry about me or my team. As always, we're prepared to handle any investigation you assign to us. If there's nothing else sir, I'd like to meet with my team to gear back up since my vacation (emphasis on the word vacation). Whether Davenport felt the sarcasm or not, he glanced back down at the paperwork on his desk and did not offer any further comment as Jeannie left his office.

She knew that Davenport would not leave this alone. If he felt that someone was dismissive with the prestige of his position, he would continue to find something to discipline her with. Thoughts of what a pompous ass Davenport was brought a smile to her face as she said goodbye.

CHAPTER 9

He watched the house and activity around it for five days. The 4th of July in this area of Delaware was enjoying a warm day for festival activities, and now the night was clear for fireworks. He doubted that the secretary at her age and health would stay awake to watch the firework displays. As for her two bodyguards, he would check on their whereabouts in the house with the night goggles.

Secretary McKinley resided in North Bethany, a very upscale neighborhood. Lower-priced houses in this area ran in the four-million-dollar range, and that was for a 2,000 square-foot home. Those that could not afford to buy a home in the area, but wanted the prestige of saying they live in North Bethany, could expect to pay around $14,500 a month in rental fees.

The information from the thumb-drive provided a complete set of floor plans for the house he would use later tonight. A three-story Tudor-style mansion: it sat on a half-acre with a gorgeous oceanfront view from all three levels with direct beach access from a private walkway. The 7,000-square-foot home had seven bedrooms suites: four bedrooms were on the second floor with the remaining three on top. The estate had four fireplaces. The expansive main level included a commercial kitchen, great room, wet bar, large solarium, screened-in porch, and a fitness room. The mansion had eight baths: three on the bottom level , three on the second level, and two on the upper level. The top level, occupied by the secretary, had a large private master-suite with spectacular vistas across the Atlantic. The grounds surrounding the estate was secured by an eight-foot iron fence with an electronically controlled massive gate blocking the driveway. The thumb drive also informed him that the occupants of the house next door would be gone for the next two weeks.

His attention this afternoon as he jogged passed the secretary's mansion was its roof gable. The mansion showed great craftsmanship and he knew that it would provide a great anchor point. He spotted several surveillance cameras at every corner and angle of the home, but none of them focused on the second or third story. The bodyguards worked eight-hour shifts with the day crew arriving for work at 8 a.m., followed by the afternoon shift at 4 p.m., and relief arriving at midnight. Each of the bodyguards wore suits and ties hiding their handguns. They appeared to be either former federal agents, law enforcement, or at least former military judging by their stature and mannerisms.

Satisfied that he completed his scouting mission, he returned to his hotel and tried to take a quick nap. Too much energy prevented him from falling into any level of sleep, so instead, he decided to take a swim in the third-floor indoor pool as well as checking out any "available" female talent. He opted to order lunch and a beer near the pool, and failing to see any females that warranted his attention, began reading the latest John Sandford paperback he picked up at the hotel gift shop. After finishing off his second beer, sleepiness began to take over, so he returned to his room and set the alarm for midnight.

CHAPTER 10

J eannie walked back to her office, and upon entering was greeted by two of her team members, Agent Ismael Flores and Agent James Burk. "Hey, Loomis. About time to get back in the thick of things. How was the 'vacation'?" asked Flores.

Jeannie had known Flores the longest of the two agents. They were both hired on the same date, but Flore's wife was expecting; so he decided with permission of the bureau to enter the FBI training facility scheduled after Jeannie. Flores was an excellent investigator, honing his skills for ten-years with the Los Angeles Police Department before applying to the Bureau. Jeannie felt that agents without prior "street smarts" did not possess the ability to handle major investigations since they seemed to lack what she called, "killer instincts."

Agent Burk, on the other hand, was extremely talented at doing paper-chases. If you had cases where money was being laundered or dummy corporations were created to hide nefarious acts, Burk was your man.

He constantly took ribbings about being more turned-on with a crime involving paper-chases that finding a hot date. Other rumors had him as a closet homosexual.

"Well, I wish I could give you both all the answers to the questions we have about the Ark investigation, but other than a long hot trip followed by a meeting with the SAC, we still don't know shit," Jeannie responded. While she spoke she felt an intense cramp below her stomach, and using her right hand pushed in on the area of discomfort. In a few seconds it passed, but her action was noticed by both agents.

"Are you OK?" asked Burk.

"Yeah, I guess my breakfast isn't sitting too well this morning," she responded.

"Anytime I have to go in and see the SAC, my stomach turns also," said Flores. Everyone laughed.

"Tell you what," Jeannie said. "Let's get out of here, have a late breakfast or early lunch at the IHOP, and you can get me caught up on our active cases. I'll tell you about my uneventful trip to Ethiopia. We can take my car so the SAC doesn't feel we're wasting gas."

During the ride over, Flores, who had more experience than Burk, gave a detailed outline of current cases they had been assigned while she was gone. None of them created any excitement in Jeannie, just your run-of-the-mill bank robberies, some small white-collar crime cases, and the usual civil rights accusations against cops just doing their job. While she was driving and asking short questions about various cases, the cramp sprang on her again. She tried to use her left hand to push in her stomach at the site of the pain without attracting attention, but Flores, sitting in the front passenger seat, appeared to notice.

They found a corner booth and thanked the waitress who brought them their menus. Flores and Burk ordered coffee with Jeannie asking for green tea. After placing their orders, Jeannie began describing her entire trip. She told them about her discussion with the hotel desk clerk, and about Nancy and Frank having stayed on two occasions at the hotel, but she could provide nothing about their disappearance. She described the chapel and her brief encounter with the guardian, and remembered she had the medal he gave her in her purse. She handed it to them, and quickly, Flores identified it as a St. Christopher necklace.

"Looks like it's been worn. Is this something the guardian gives everyone?" Flores asked.

"I didn't see him give anything to anyone else while I was there," Jeannie responded.

"Hum, maybe he just liked your looks," said Flores with a smile on his face.

"You're such a pervert. He's a man of the cloth." She replied.

"Yeah, but he's a man," Flores countered. I bet if you showed him a little skin or swayed your ass he might have told you a lot of stuff." Flores started laughing at what he had said, only to get a hard stare from Jeannie, which turned into a smile while shaking her head.

CHAPTER 11

It was easy to disarm the house alarm system next to the secretary's mansion. Sitting there throughout the day, he continued to monitor the mansion next door. The only lights that came on were landscaping illumination. There was a quarter-moon which added to his camouflage. He was dressed in black, including his normal vintage navy facemask. He preferred this style of mask since he had modified the mouth area by punched holes that allowed him to breathe in and out a lot easier than a version completely covering that area. No matter how much planning, the excitement and adrenalin rush that overcame him during a kill required him to suck in a lot of air.

The sky, although dark, seemed to have a purple hue. Maybe it was caused by too much backyard BBQ smoke, he thought. He could smell smoke in the air, and since there was no wind, the air seemed heavier than the previous night. As predicted, some delayed 4th of July fireworks sporadically exploded, generally coming from the beach area.

It was an easy climb to the roof area of the adjacent home. Over his shoulder he had his backpack containing the equipment he felt necessary to carry out the job. He pulled out the night vision goggles and began doing a floor by floor viewing of the secretary's mansion. No one was visible on the second floor. Two individuals, presumably bodyguards, were sitting near the front door entrance off to the side of the vestibule. Their lack of movement suggested they were watching television.

On the third floor, he saw the secretary laying in a bed. The time was 12:11 a.m., July 5th. He needed to wait until 1 a.m., giving him enough time to watch the movement of the bodyguards and pick up any pattern they might have while working their shift. Now all he could do was lay out the Zipcord line and the gun modified to fire the Zipline anchor. He patted his breast pocket for the bottle of Chloroform and the rag. Check.

There were only two movements involving the bodyguards. Both, at different times, had gotten up to use the first level bathroom. This was followed by one of them walking the outside and inside perimeter of the mansion. He then returned to the same area of the bottom floor, possibly returning to a movie or late-night show on the television with his partner. How can people watch such crap he thought? Meanwhile, while observing the secretary, he noted she only tossed in her sleep one time.

1 a.m. Time to "play," he thought. He loaded the Zipline anchor into the modified pistol and aimed at the roof gable. Holding his breath while wishing for a fireworks explosion, he fired the gun. No fireworks went off when he fired, but at almost the exact second the anchor penetrated the gable and grabbed hold, a bottle rocket or something similar exploded over the ocean. The brilliant light briefly lit up the roof area where he was standing, but only for a fraction of a second.

He waited a few minutes so he could check on the two bodyguards. They did not move. Next, he checked on the secretary. She did not stir. Just as planned, he thought. Now came the fun stuff: he put on his leather gloves and reached for the main equipment needed for the next phase of his adventure.

He put on the Zipline harness and attached the trolley to the line. He had meticulously considered the slope, wind speed, temperature, weight, friction, and speed. In this case, the slope was uphill from the adjacent house where he perched. He determined that he would need a brake to slow his return trip from the higher elevation. The trip over would easily take longer than the trip back after completing the job. He remembered reading somewhere: "It's about the journey and not the destination." That thought brought a smile to his face. Time for the next phase.

CHAPTER 12

H e grabbed the Zipline, and after testing to see if it would support his weight and the anchor was secure, he held onto the Trolley and stepped off the roof. He slowly made his ascent to the secretary's roof and knelt down, listening for any sounds. Hearing nothing, he removed the harness and checked the anchor. Since the roof gable could not be seen by anyone looking up from any of the bedroom windows, the anchor would remain behind. Once he retreated to the anchor neighbor's house, with a strong tug, he could pull the Zipcord line free and retrieve it.

Luckily, the secretary had left the bedroom windows open due to the heat and humidity. Piece of cake, he thought. He climbed through the window watching the sleeping secretary. Still no movement. He walked over to the bed and stared down on her. The peacefully sleeping woman who could be the poster image of the ideal grandma, was one of the most corrupt females in the nation. Educated at an Ivy League university, she swallowed the ideology of

Saul Alinsky and his *Rules for Radicals*. He could go on with more condemnations of the secretary, but why waste his time and energy. Soon, she would be no more.

He removed the small bottle of Chloroform and rag from his breast pocket. He poured a generous amount on the rag and slowly started a descent onto the secretary's mouth and nose area. He allowed her to breathe the fumes while holding the rag one-inch above her. He kept his head turned. Noticing that her breathing was slowing down, he placed the rag firmly over her nose and mouth. Glancing at his watch, he noted the passing of five-minutes and then removed the rag. She never moved during the whole event. He forcibly shook her, but got no response. None was anticipated; if she had awakened, he would have quickly applied the rag again.

Now the heavy part. He did not feel that the secretary weighed very much, but dealing with dead weight is not as easy as Hollywood depicts it. He grabbed her right arm and pulled her to the right side of the bed, slowly pulling her body onto the floor, making as little sound as he could. He waited and listened. Nothing from the bodyguards. Now with her on the floor, he retrieved her slippers and placed one on her left foot, tucking the right slipper into his back pocket. He slowly dragged the secretary towards the bedroom door, lowered her to the floor and slowly opened the door hoping it would not squeak. It did not. He opened it as wide as possible and then walked silently to the staircase. The stairs were covered with a very plush ivory-colored rug. Taking his knife, he pulled a small part of the rug from the tack strip-- just enough so that upon inspection, someone would conclude it contributed to her fall. One stair below this area, he strategically placed the right slipper at a forty-five-degree angle.

He retrieved the secretary by grabbing her from behind and stood her in an upright position, supporting her weight. He waddled silently to the top of the stairs, and after taking a deep breath, let her go. He could hear a loud thumping sound as the secretary tumbled down the stairs.

Without wasting time, he climbed out the window and hoisted himself up to the roof. He quickly put on his harness and grabbed the trolley. The return trip was awesome, with thoughts flashing of young Kevin zipping to the treehouse as he made his escape from the bungling burglars in *Home Alone*. The zip brake worked flawlessly. With one hard pull, he freed the line from the anchor and he was lying on the neighbor's roof, as quiet as he could be. A few minutes later, he heard emergency vehicles racing to the scene. He continued to watch from his position.

After what seemed like at least ten-minutes, one of the bodyguards was seen at the window that had just been used for the assassin's escape. The bodyguard looked outside and then went to the second and third window and perform the same task. Nothing to see, the assassin thought.

He gathered up his equipment and placed it in his backpack, making his way from the roof and walking toward his awaiting vehicle in the opposite direction of the secretary's house. He placed the equipment in the trunk, and before he got into the driver's seat he was amazed by another beautiful firework exploding over the ocean. Happy 4th of July, he thought. Oh, wait; it's now July 5th.

CHAPTER 13

Jeannie, Flores, Ismael and Burk finished their meal and were preparing to leave the IHOP when a young college aged female walked up to their table, focused on Burk. "Hello, I thought that was you," she said.

"Hi, how are you?" Burk answered while standing up and hugging her.

Jeannie looked at Flores and they both broke out in a smile at the same time.

"Cindy, this is Jeannie and Ismael, colleagues of mine," he said. Looking at Jeannie and Ismael he said, "Cindy was my old computer lab partner at the University."

"Hello," and "Nice to meet you" greetings were exchanged, followed by Burk asking Cindy how she had been? Turning to Jeannie and Ismael, Burk apologized and said that they should return to work, and that he would catch a taxi or Uber and get back as soon as he and Cindy caught up on things since it had been years since seeing one another.

Jeannie and Ismael agreed. Both said, "Nice to meet you" to Cindy and walked out of the restaurant.

"Well, maybe the rumors aren't correct," Ismael said.

Predisposed in her thoughts, Jeannie asked, "What rumors?"

"The rumors that Burk is still in the closet."

"Gee, you guys worry about anything related to sex, don't you?" Jeannie asked, not expecting a response.

Ismael just laughed, but noticed that Jeannie had placed her left hand on her stomach region like before. "When are you going to tell me?" he asked.

"Tell you what?" she said while blushing.

"Tell you what? Tell me you're pregnant, that's what," he responded.

"Pregnant! Who said I'm pregnant. Did you get your MD license while I was in Ethiopia?

"Look, lady, I have five kids, five!" while holding up five fingers. "I'm what the Portuguese call a 'breeding machine.' Don't you think a man can tell the signs when a woman is pregnant? Right now, you're experiencing cramps, right?" Not waiting for an answer, he continued, "Soon you'll get nauseous at things you try to eat, or even some odors. I know, my wife used to love to make sopas. It's a Portuguese dish where you cook pot roast for a long time with mint, onion, garlic, cinnamon, allspice, and bay leaves and then pour the juice over French bread. She could put two or three pieces of bread and a ton of meat away and never get fat. Then as soon as she gets pregnant, bam, just the smell of the spices, and she's upchucking for days. I know when a woman is pregnant. Remember, I'm an FBI agent." With this, he smiles.

"All right, damn it. I don't think I'm pregnant, but the cramps have gotten worse, so I went to Kaiser and saw my doctor yesterday. This had better stay between you and me. Got that?"

"Hey, my lips are sealed," Ismael said while staring straight ahead at the heavier than usual traffic passing by the federal buildings. Then he asked, and she knew it was coming. "Who's the father? Anyone, I know?"

"No one you know, and like I said, I don't think I'm pregnant."

CHAPTER 14

"**J**eannie Loomis," the female nursing assistant paged to a crowd of patients seated in the waiting room area for Medical Station Two, at the Kaiser Hospital. Jeannie rose at the sound of her name and walked toward the young-looking nurse.

"Hi, how are you today?" asked the nurse.

"Fine," Jeannie stated as she handed the nurse the standard questionnaire asking not only personal medical questions but also private stuff such as, "Have you been abused at home? etc." The nursing assistant took the clipboard that held Jeannie's questionnaire, not looking at the sheet. She told Jeannie they would be in examination room four and requested that Jeannie follow her.

Arriving at the room, the nurse told Jeannie she could put her personal belongings, which in her case was simply her purse, on a chair and motioned to a GYN table that was in an upright position. Jeannie sat on the end of the table, hateing what she knew would follow.

"So, you don't remember when you had your last menstrual period?" the nurse asked.

"Not really. I've been so busy, it just doesn't register to me when it last occurred." Jeannie replied.

"I understand," said the nurse in a manner that hinted she had heard this response numerous times. After taking Jeannie's blood pressure and temperature, and putting the pertinent information into the computer mounted to the wall opposite the GYN table, she instructed Jeannie to remove all her clothing and to dress in a non-fashionable paper gown. She then said that Doctor Morrow would be in shortly.

She wished she had asked the nurse for her definition of "shortly," because, thirty-five minutes later she was still waiting for the doctor's arrival, freezing her ass off.

Finally, Doctor Morrow arrived. "Hello, I'm Doctor Morrow. I'm so sorry I'm late. No matter how they try to schedule our rounds, we always seem to fall a little behind." While saying what Jeannie felt was a standard line all doctors use, the doctor put out her hand and a handshake was shared.

Dr. Morrow, without saying anything further, looked at Jeannie's chart.

"OK, I see it's been over five years since you've had a physical. Any illnesses during that time?" she asked.

"No, just a minor cold here and there, and sometimes a little allergy headache; but, I've felt great," Jeannie responded. "I'm sure that the cramps

I've been having are due to the strain and stress I've been under the last few months," she added.

"What has caused the stress for you?" the doctor asked.

"Doctor, I'm an FBI agent and, well, stress is just part of the job. I'm sure you understand."

"Of course, of course. So, you're here because you've been experiencing menstrual cramps, but you don't recall your last period. Is that correct?"

"Yes, I've been so involved in this one particular case that I frankly cannot recall when I had my last period, but I know it's been at least two months," Jeannie said.

"Stress and even heavy exercise can sometimes mess up one's cycle. Have you been sexually active during this time?" the doctor probed.

Jeannie could feel the redness rise from her chest up to her forehead and knew that the doctor had noticed her embarrassment.

"Yes, a few times," Jeannie offered, trying to convey there weren't many; but, the doctor would not give up.

"How many would you say, and have you been practicing safe sex?

Jeannie, feeling her blushing go to an even higher intensity level, trying to keep her latest blackout "relationship" secret, lied and said, "Maybe three." Her thoughts quickly turned to a self-examination mode where she could not believe she had spiraled out of control to the point of not remembering how many men she had been with, much less, their names.

"Please let me lower the table so I can give you an exam," the doctor said. Jeannie stood while the doctor lowered the table. She then asked Jeannie to lay down and put her feet in the stirrups.

The examination did not take very long, and the doctor stated that she did not find anything of note. She told Jeannie that she was ordering a blood and urine test at the lab and she could stop on her way out and get that completed. The results would be emailed to her.

CHAPTER 15

J udge Harold Kavanaugh was the presiding judge during this session of the Star Chamber. No member had direct knowledge of how long the other judges had been on the Star Chamber court. Judge Kavanaugh was much older than Katamoto, so many assumed he had been on the Star Chamber court a long time. Completely bald with an obviously dyed mustache, he placed a lot of fear in the minds of defense attorneys that had their cases assigned to his normal Superior Court department. Being on the bench for over thirty-five years with retirement in the wings, he didn't give a shit about some of his rulings being overturned by the appellate court. By the time the defense applied for a new hearing, he would be retired. They could kiss his ass.

As the other judges took their respective seats, he turned on the computer and displayed a picture of billionaire Horace Beaumont on the television screen. Several judges had a scornful look on their face, and a few f-bombs were quietly expressed. One judge even stated out loud that Beaumont's whole family should be eliminated.

Judge Kavanaugh was a lot less polished than Katamoto in how he presided over the Star Chamber, similar to how he conducted himself in his normal courtroom; he was a no nonsense jurist.

"OK, gentlemen," he began, glancing to both sides of the curved table. "The defendant is Horace Beaumont. I'll introduce evidence to the court showing that the defendant financially supports at least three urban terrorists' groups here in the United States as well as finances two global networks. I'll also show that the defendant is extremely secretive in his terrorist funding activities, always distancing himself and organization from direct connections.

Beaumont had made his money the old fashion way. He inherited it. Some say it goes back to the time of Prohibition. There are even rumors that he'd found some stolen Nazi gold. Regardless of his billions coming from oil, gold, silver, booze, prostitution, embezzlement or blackmail, he's one of the top ten billionaires in the world. An ultra-liberal, he espouses the virtue of a global community and hates all forms of democracy. His terrorist groups show up at major political events, not to protest, but to use Nazi brown-shirt like tactics--causing injury, property destruction, and even death.

After the most recent election, fearing for his life, he relocated with his family to the Swiss Alps where he lives in a spectacular historic chateau. Even though he holds two passports, he's not flown to the United States since November."

Judge Kavanaugh proceeded to lay out the evidence in an orderly manner and upon conclusion asked the other judges if they had any questions. He then addressed the court with his closing arguments:

"The defendant, Horace Beaumont has been accused of financing terrorist activity both in the United States as well as in France, Belgium, and Spain. He is indirectly responsible for the injury of hundreds and the death of thirteen individuals. The property destruction of his groups exceeds three million dollars. Meanwhile, he hides with his family in his Swiss Alps chateau evading justice from the United States."

Upon concluding his closing arguments, Judge Kavanaugh asked the other eight judges if they had any questions. Receiving none, he stated that he would now proceed to a polling of the jurists. He picked up a laminated three-by-four inch card and read the following verbatim:

"The defendant, Horace Beaumont, has been accused of terrorism both domestically and internationally. Only upon a unanimous verdict by this court, will sentencing be pronounced. At this time I will poll the court. I will now call the roll for your verdict.

"Judge Roberts?"

"Guilty."

"Judge Swartz?"

"Guilty."
"Judge Baldwin?"
"Guilty."
"Judge Kalford?"
"Guilty."
"Judge Katamoto?"
"Guilty."
"Judge Hall?"
"Guilty."
"Judge Silverman?"
"Guilty."
"Judge Henderson?"
"Guilty."

"At this time, I will enter my judgment which is guilty. We have a unanimous verdict of Guilt -Level One Sentence. I make the motion to notify the SDL for immediate execution of our verdict. All in favor say aye."

"Aye!" was the response.

"Sergeant of Arms. Please notify SDL of our decision." With that, the judge struck the walnut base with his gavel and announced that the court was adjourned.

CHAPTER 16

Jeannie sat in one of the few Dutch Brothers coffee shops that had an interior for customers to sit and enjoy their drinks. Stirring her green tea, she contemplated her pending blood test results. I can't be pregnant, she thought. How can I be a mother? What about my job? She felt she was blushing as she realized the jokes that will be made behind her back about getting knocked-up and having no idea as to who the father is. She knew Davenport would have a field day with this. She had thought about buying one of those self-pregnancy test kits, but thought it would be better to wait until results came from a medical professional.

A customer across from her was placing his coffee cup in the trash can and his newspaper on the shelf above. He then walked out the door. Jeannie got up and grabbed the newspaper before anyone else had the opportunity. She glanced at the headlines.

"*Former U.S. Secretary Dead,*" the headlines read. The article went on to read that the former U.S.

Secretary of State, Virginia McKenzie, seventy years old, died early that morning in what authorities say appeared to be a fall down a flight of stairs. The secretary was immediately found by her security team who heard her fall and ran to her location. They called 911 and attempted to resuscitate her. She was declared dead at the scene.

Jeannie turned to the sports section to see how her San Francisco Giants were doing. Born and raised in the Bay Area, she and her family had loved and followed the Giants for years. She experienced their string of successes, winning the World Series in 2010, 2012 and 2014.

Her cellphone rang, and seeing that it was from SAC Davenport, she thought that her day was going to start bad.

"Loomis," she answered.

"Loomis, I need to see you and your team as soon as possible," he said.

"OK, I'm already on the way in and they should all be there soon," she replied.

Davenport did not respond; he just hung up. What an asshole, she thought. She hit speed dialing and reached both Burk and Flores to made sure they were, in fact, on their way to the office. Both of them asked if she knew what the SAC wanted, and she told them she knew as much as them, which was nothing.

She first went to her office and made short contact with Flores and Burk. Together, the three grabbed the elevator to the sixth floor and were greeted by Davenport's secretary, Stephanie. Stephanie had confided in Jeannie that she had put in for a transfer since she could not stand Davenport and his personality; but so far, she had not heard anything about her request. She felt that Davenport knew though, because he was acting more and more like a pompous ass.

Stephanie knocked on Davenport's door and upon opening it, told him that Agent Loomis and her team were there. Without looking at her, Davenport made a hand motion to let them in.

The three entered Davenport's office. Only two chairs were facing his desk, so all three decided to just stand until he gave them his attention. Fifteen seconds of silence passed before he looked up at all three agents and said, "This is confidential and stays in this room." He then grabbed a file from the left side of his desk and opened it.

"The bureau has received an anonymous letter containing some incriminating evidence, including photos, of criminal activity involving a Judge named George Baldwin.

Baldwin presides as a Superior Court judge in New Castle County, Delaware. The letter implicates Judge Baldwin in not only trafficking child pornography online, but having traveled abroad as a guest of Michael Cartwright known for sex orgies with females as young as eleven. Anyway, it's all in this file." As he began handing the file to Jeannie, and as she started to reach across his desk to retrieve it, Davenport pulled it back. He stared at Jeannie and said the case was of particular interest to top administration and had to be handled discreetly, and with utmost discretion. Then, as if to pour vinegar into a wound, he looked at Jeannie and then at both Flores and Burk saying, "I hope I don't get a repeat of your last investigation."

Jeannie, knowing from years of working with Flores, immediately sensed that he was about to verbally explode on Davenport. She grabbed Flores's arm and then the file and said, "We won't sir," in a sarcastic, but respectful manner that Davenport did not seem to notice. They retreated from his office and reconvened in the team room. Flores thanked Jeannie for stopping him. "That son-of-a-bitch Davenport," he said.

CHAPTER 17

S he checked into the five-star hotel nestled in the Alps, next to the Andermatt train station and Nätschen ski lift. At the heart of the Swiss Alps, it was 1,447 meters above sea level. It had 123 rooms and suites, four award-winning restaurants and bars and a modern health club and spa area. More importantly, it was extremely close to her target's residence. She had booked a deluxe room versus a suite. Always a frugal one, why waste your money when you are just going to shower and sleep in the room, she reasoned. Who knew, she thought, she might have some time before and after her big event to get in some skiing.

She was twenty-eight years old but could easily pass as a sixteen to eighteen-year-old. Sandy colored hair dropped passed her shoulders, and freckles speckled her nose. Both ears were pierced, but unlike some of her friends, she refused to wear a ring through her lip. She accepted the fact that God gave her a boy's body. She was lucky to fill a 30C bra and that was generally when she was having her period. Taller than most of her female friends, she stood at 5'7" and had a female athletic body. She remembered breaking the nose of a dude who called her a transgender male.

She found a site near the hotel that rented snowmobiles and told the attendant she was an experienced snowmobile enthusiast not needing instructions on how to operate the vehicle. She signed the paperwork, promised to return the machine before dusk, and set off to the east. East: the location of her target.

Beaumont's estate was perched on a mountain top with only one road that granted access and egress--not a problem for what she had planned. The building was only two stories high, but where it stood it gave the impression of a large castle floating in the sky, especially when fog rose to the base of the main structure. To the right of where she stopped the snowmobile, was a stand of large trees which she felt could be used for concealment purposes. While she continued to evaluate the target's home, other people raced up and down the rolling hills on their snowmobiles, the sound of their engines echoing through the canyons. Perfect, she thought.

She returned the snowmobile and visited a small bakery nearby, buying a hot mocha and two caracs that were even better than the ones available in her home town of Grindelwald. She ate them while walking towards a gathering of people watching a group, mostly children, ice skate. While watching, she noticed a male wearing a red and blue ski cap place a dark plastic bag on a bench. He stood next to the bag until he saw her walking towards him. He was gone in the crowd before she retrieved the bag. Picking it up as if it had always belonged to her, she returned to watching the children ice skate. She had learned how to ice skate when she was a small child, but preferred ice hockey.

Back in her room, she placed the plastic bag on her bed. She then opened her backpack and took out her modified drone, inspecting it, and was pleased no damage had occurred during its transport. Using a note pad and pen gratuitously provided by the hotel and lying by the phone, she began to list in order what was left to do. She glanced at her watch to note the time and folded the paper she had written on, shoving it into her bra. What the hell she thought, there's plenty of room there.

Before leaving, she opened the bag and found a small vial needed for her assignment. She opened the mini-bar and placed the object between the bottles of Sommerbier and La Verte beer. Even if someone like a thieving maid found the object, she doubted they would know what it was. But, if they opened it, well, they would release hell.

CHAPTER 18

Michael Cartwright was a multi-millionaire pervert. A Pedophile, flesh trafficker, drug dealer, fence of top-end jewelry and art, he was buddy-buddy with many politicians, actors, judges, sports figures, and the social elite. It was rumored that he had an island somewhere near Jamaica where he would satisfy the sexual appetite of these well-known celebrities, regardless of how deprived it might be—even providing jets to fly them in. Underaged boys and girls were the prizes they received when they arrived. No costs were involved; no money exchanged hands.

Some say he made his money by working with a drug cartel out of Mexico. Others think he just skimed his share off the top while fencing jewelry and art, allowed him to amass a fortune. All of his income was generated through criminal activity.

Today, he was in his office in New York, posing as a hedge fund manager. Of course, there was no fund and he was not a manager. No, today he was arranging for the next island party and calling invitees to arrange the trip.

"Hello, may I speak to Judge Baldwin, please? Michael Cartwright calling." The female who answered the phone, presumably a maid, said, "Just a moment sir."

"Hello, Michael. How have you been? I was hoping you would call," Judge Baldwin stated after answering the call.

"Fine, your honor. Hey, are you free on the evening of August 22nd to fly to our normal destination for a little R & R? That's a Friday evening and we'll return Sunday around noon. That gives you two nights to relax.

"Michael, two great minds think alike. Thank you so much for the invite. Will my young 'friends' be waiting?"

"Oh yes, I don't think you'll be disappointed. Shall I send a car to pick you up and drive you to the airport, say at 4 p.m.?" Cartwright asked.

"That would be great. Shit, I'm so excited, I've already got a hard-on," Judge Baldwin said.

"Guess I'll need to fire up the computer and relieve myself since Friday's seven days away. See you on Friday my friend."

"Yes, Judge, see you on Friday." And with that, Cartwright hung up.

"OK, we got all that, right?" asked Jeannie looking at Burk and the recording equipment on his desk.

"Crystal, what a sleez bag," he responded.

"What now? Asked Flores.

"First, I want to contact Interpol and give Agent Delaney what we have. They could work the Cartwright--sex island angle. It would be great to bust Cartwright's little empire and save those children. I'd like to get a look at the names of all those perverts that Cartwright has invited to these orgies." Jeannie paused, but during the pause, Flores said, "Hey, maybe Davenport is on the list."

Jeannie smiled and said, "Next, we run what we have so far through legal tomorrow morning and see if we have enough for a search warrant for Judge Baldwins' computer. It could be a treasure trove for us, and who knows where it could lead."

Five o'clock arrived, and the three departed the building.

Jeannie stopped at a Subway and was going to buy a six-inch chicken & bacon ranch melt but felt extremely hungry, so instead got a "foot-long." She decided on the meal special which included a bag of chips and a fountain drink. Damn, her bra was tight for some reason, she thought, need to get some new ones—wondering when she bought new underwear.

When she arrived home, she put the food on her kitchen counter and went to the restroom. After relieving herself she went to the bedroom, kicked off her shoes, and took off her blouse, bra and pants. She put the bra on the floor next to her clothes hamper with the intent of throwing it away, and also as a reminder to get some new underwear. She found her favorite Giants t-shirt and a pair of shorts, put them on, and returned to the kitchen.

Immediately upon opening the bag of potato chips, she felt nauseous with an intense urge to vomit. She ran to the bathroom and as quickly as she could, opened the lid to the toilet. She started to experience dry heaves, which brought on more cramps. What seemed like forever, she slowly righted herself and even though she never really upchucked, she wiped her mouth with a washcloth and looked into the bathroom mirror. The thought of being pregnant raced through her mind, but the cramping could also mean her period was about to start, right?

Feeling a little better, she went back into the kitchen. Trying not to inhale any smells from the bag of potato chips, she put them and the submarine sandwich in her refrigerator. She kept the diet Coke and sat down on her couch, turning on the television. A newswoman was seen standing in what presumably was the late Secretary of State's residence.

"Law enforcement is wrapping up their investigation into the accidental death of former Secretary of State, Virginia McKenzie. The respective former secretary slipped on a loose portion of the rug covering a stair and tumbled to her death. No foul play is suspected."

"Respected my ass," Jeannie said to the television set. "If I did one-tenth of what the bitch and her late husband did, I'd be in federal prison for at least thirty years. Respected, bullshit?" while shaking her head. Shit, now she was getting a headache. Might as well call it an early evening and head to bed.

CHAPTER 19

She woke at dawn, had a continental breakfast and rented a snowmobile. She wanted to be inside the tree line before other snowmobile enthusiasts were out and about and before anyone in the Beaumont house awakened. In her pocket, was a well wrapped vial of VX-gas. She knew the deadly coincidences of being exposed to this nerve agent; but, she also knew that it was exponentially deadlier when warmed up. She had practiced numerous times with a vial filled with a liquid equivalent in weight to VX-gas mounted to her drone with success. She attached the VX-gas vial to the drone. Then, taking a common cigarette lighter began heating the glass container.

As she was warming the VX, she remembered during her research that it was developed in the United Kingdom back in the early 1950s. It is odorless and tasteless. Following the release of VX into the air, people can be exposed through skin contact, eye contact, or inhalation (breathing in the VX mist), thus the heating of the vial. Because VX vapor is heavier than air, it will sink to low-lying areas and create a greater exposure hazard there.

That should do it, she thought. She started up the drone. In the distance, she could hear a few snowmobiles, but so far none near her location. The drone rose from the ground and started its climb to Beaumont's chateau. She had to constantly adjust for wind variations, but that was expected.

Feeling that the bedrooms were located on the second floor, she chose a window near the center. The drone flew flawlessly towards that location, but she did have to compensate for the occasional wind shear. Hovering for a brief minute, she decided it was now time to meet her client or client's demand.

At the precise moment, she directed the drone to the window. The drone had enough speed and weight to easily break the glass and enter the building. She was too far away to hear the crash or screams that should be filling the house now. The vial would break on impact as she had seen happen on practice exercises, and spread through the chateau. Those that ran to the scene of the crash would be exposed. Those away from that particular bedroom would soon be overcome by the gas. The exposed should be experiencing convulsions, loss of consciousness, paralysis, respiratory failure, and then death. She waited thirty-minutes to make sure no one exited the building, allowing the gas to do its work. Satisfied that no one suspected what had happened, she left the tree line and returned the snowmobile. Her job was done.

CHAPTER 20

J eannie arrived at the bureau before either Flores or Burk. She went directly to legal to see what the decision was regarding the search warrant request. If legal felt a warrant would be granted, they had to use a court outside the jurisdiction of Judge Baldwin, and it had to be signed by a judge who did not know him. Jeannie learned it had been granted and was expected to return from the court by 10 a.m. Her cellphone rang and upon checking it she saw a phone number for Kaiser Permanente. Oh God, she thought.

First, she needed to brief the SAC. That thought alone made her nauseous. Stephanie greeted her as always and after knocking and checking with Davenport, directed Jeannie to his office. She stood versus taking a seat, and as customary waited for him to recognize her presence. Without looking up he said, "Take a seat." She complied.

"What do we have with Judge Baldwin?" he asked.

"We have the transcript of a phone call between Baldwin and Cartwright in which he accepts the invite to what we are calling the 'sex island party' near Jamaica. In the conversation, he talks about his preference for young boys and girls."

Davenport raised his right-hand requesting Jeannie to stop. "You do realize we have no jurisdiction in Jamaica, correct?"

"Yes, at the conclusion of the phone call he implicates himself in the use of underage pornography that he has on his personal computer. I ran it past legal and they felt there was enough for a search warrant which should be ready by 10 a.m. today."

"Legal has already approved it? And a judge has signed off on it?" he asked.

"Yes, Sir."

Davenport paused and tapped his left fingers on paperwork lying on the desk.

"OK, I don't want you to execute the search warrant until after 5 p.m. today since it's a Friday, and by the time the press gets wind of it, their deadline will have passed. That way, if there's a screw-up we'll have the weekend to do damage control. Remember who we're dealing with and the orders I got from above. Everything must be by the book."

What do you know about working "by the book?" What a prick. He took advantage of any way he could insult her indirectly--by referring to the failure of the Ark investigation. God, Jeannie thought, wouldn't it be great if somehow Davenport was caught in what should become a sensational sex scandal? No, he was too shrewd to get caught up in something like that. Political blackmail, maybe, but not something like this.

CHAPTER 21

J eannie picked up the signed search warrant and headed back to her office. Her cellphone binged, indicating she had received a text. It was from a scheduling nurse at Kaiser, asking her to call for an appointment at her earliest convenience. "Have to wait," Jeannie said to herself.

Flores and Burk were already in her office where a floor plan of Judge's Baldwin's home was displayed on one of the walls. Someone guessed which room probably contained his computer and indicated it by circling the room with a red marker. Of course, if the Judge had a laptop, there would be no need for a dedicated computer room. But, Jeannie thought, someone showed some initiative.

On her desk was a mocha from Dutch Bros, her favorite. She grabbed the cup and pulled off the top, but as soon as she smelled the aroma of the brew, she felt a little queasy and put the top back on. "I'll drink this later," she said, trying to squelch this bout of nausea, and continued. "The SAC wants us to hold off executing the search warrant until after 5 p.m. so that if anything goes wrong, the media will have to contend with their deadlines, and it being a weekend....etc. Since the Judge lives alone, I've only requested three other agents to join, which should be adequate. He does own two registered handguns, so be aware. OK, go home and get some sleep and be back here at 3:30 sharp so that we can plan our approach with the other agents."

Flores and Burk left her office and after taking a seat, she pulled out her cellphone. She dialed, and after three rings was greeted by a cheerful female asking for her name and Kaiser ID number. She confirmed her date of birth, and when asked what the receptionist could help her with, said she was returning a message from a scheduling nurse whose name she could not recall.

"Oh yes, I see here that Dr. Morrow would like to set up an appointment with you. She currently has next Tuesday at 10:15 open, or 3:30 the same day."

"Sorry, but right now neither of those times work due to work commitments. Did she indicate the results of my blood test?" Jeannie asked.

"No, I'm sorry. I only see on the computer and her request to set up an appointment with you," she replied.

"OK, let me call you back tomorrow when I have a clearer idea of my workload and then I'll see what dates and times Dr. Morrow has open."

"That's fine. Have a nice day."

"You too," Jeannie replied. Huh, maybe it is against policy to give a patient any type of medical information like, "Hey, you're pregnant, congratulations!" Jeannie secured the search warrant in her desk drawer and headed home.

CHAPTER 22

J eannie was preoccupied with the nature of the phone call with the Kaiser representative and finally shook it off by turning on the car radio.

"...... *Swiss authorities will only confirm that three people, including billionaire Horace Beaumont, died in his mountain chateau. Their bodies were found late yesterday evening when phone calls were not being returned. The cause of death has not been announced. Beaumont, eighty-seven years old, was said to be in excellent health for his age. He financed many progressive groups as well as making major contributions to global initiative issues and global warming...*"

Couldn't happen to a better asshole Jeannie thought as she opted for a CD of ABBA. She began singing to *Dancing Queen* while trying to anticipate any problems she and her team might encounter this evening. She thought she had anticipated everything that could go wrong, but she had been in the business too long to realize that was impossible. She remembered that she had the Subway sandwich from last night in the refrigerator and felt that a quick cool shower, sandwich, ice tea, and a nap, would get her ready for this evening's adventure.

While falling asleep, she recalled the death of Beaumont. Another asshole bites the dust she thought. I wonder who else was in the house? His son was a piece-of-shit also and his third wife was a left-wing wacko. With those thoughts, Jeannie fell asleep.

The alarm she had placed on the coffee table near the couch went off at 3 PM. Experiencing apparent night sweats, she again jumped into the shower. She had been able to eat most of the sub and was not experiencing any more nausea or dry heaves. But, at the same time, she had not started her period. Got to make that damn appointment with Dr. Morrow and stop dicking around, she thought. First thing tomorrow, without fail.

Burk and one other agent, Wilson, had already arrived by the time Jeannie entered her office. She knew Wilson and said "hi," thanking him for volunteering. By 4 o'clock, everyone arrived, and Jeannie asked Flores to explain the case and plan of attack. After laying out the crimes Judge Baldwin was suspected of committing, he emphasized that Judge Baldwin had access to two registered handguns. Once contact was made, he needed to be searched for weapons and then secured in a room with agent Wilson.

Burk would secure all computers found in the house. One of the two assisting agents would videotape the search and retrieval of evidence. The other agent would help in the general search of the rest of the residence. Jeannie asked if anyone had questions. No one did. She looked at the clock which read 4:45.

"Ok, its time. Be careful out there," and with that Jeannie walked with her team to their respective vehicles. Everyone realized that officers get killed when they underestimate the danger of their job, especially, assuming that violence was not expected in this type of search warrant. But, if any evidence was found of underage sexual activity including the possession of child-porn, Judge Baldwin's career was over.

CHAPTER 23

The sergeant-at-arms announced the court was in session. Judge Henderson lightly struck the gavel to the base and the room became silent. Much like other alternating presiding judges, Henderson turned on the television set to display the night's defendant, but two photos appeared instead.

"This is Daniel Blackstone: twenty-eight years old. He's the leader of a group of anti-fascists who organize protests in response to right-wing rallies most recently in Portland, Oregon, and Berkeley, California. As usual with these types of individuals, he stays in the rear while orchestrating brutal attacks on peaceful activists. In the Portland incident, two elderly individuals were bludgeoned to death by his thugs, while in Berkeley, fourteen individuals were seriously injured with property damage running over $800,000 last count. Reliable sources in the law enforcement communities of both cities say that they were ordered to "stand-down" by their administrators." Some comments could be heard from a few of the judges.

A second photo appeared of a middle-aged black female wearing glasses that were in fashion back in the 1960s. "If you don't know, this is Summer Tillson, Esq. Another far left-leaning attorney spawned from the days of the hippy movement. Tillson is believed to be financed by none other than Horace Beaumont (more grumbling emanating in the room). A former professor of law and now an activist, she defends not only Blackstone, but at least eight other domestic-terrorists groups. This is the same lawyer who was unsuccessfully prosecuted in 2002 for smuggling a handgun into a maximum-security prison, resulting in the death of two correctional officers. A technicality got her off. In this photo, you can see her in a coffee shop meeting with Blackstone. Here she's handing him an envelope, which was later confirmed, contained currency." He advances to the next picture.

"This is a newspaper advertisement placed by Blackstone ten-days before the incident in Portland, offering employment to picket an upcoming lecture given by a famous conservative talk show host. It offers $20 per hour for approximately five hours of work." He clicked on the presenter and a picture showing Blackstone and Tillson meeting at the same coffee shop.

"Here, ten days before the riot in Berkeley, you see the same transaction take place between the two. Intelligence officers of Portland and Berkeley sought a search warrant allowing them to wiretap both Blackstone and Tillson. Since all they had was circumstantial information, no wiretap was granted. I should add that they came to my chambers requesting the warrant, but as you fellow judges are aware, I couldn't grant their request." Judge Henderson paused and poured some water into a glass and drank it. He then continued.

"Per our bylaws, I polled Judges Swartz and Kanamoto and we unanimously decided a wiretap was warranted. The SDL monitored both Tillson and Blackstone for two weeks. From their conversations we learned they're planning another riot on September 11 in Dallas, Texas, where a pro-administration rally will be held. Here's some of the audio:

'I received the funds yesterday. He wants a bigger crowd on hand and wants more dressed in Antifa style. As before, you can tell your recruit, that if they're arrested, legal fees will be paid for them. In other words, he doesn't want them to hold back.'" Judge Henderson indicated the female voice was that of Tillson.

"That shouldn't be a problem. Offering $20 an hour for such a short period of time makes it easy to recruit. I'll warn you, however, that the Dallas cops will probably not be ordered to stand down, so there'll be injuries."

"That's the voice of Blackstone," said Judge Henderson.

"He wants a lot of confrontation and anarchy. His words," Tillson replied.

"Hey, with his money, he can get whatever he wants. Let the mayhem begin! See you at the usual spot tomorrow morning so I can get the funds. Is that OK with you?"

"That's fine. See you there," at which point, both hung up.

Judge Henderson finished his presentation and asked the other jurists for questions or comments. Judge Kalford informed the other judges that he had Tillson practice in his courtroom. "She is a very militant, disruptive, arrogant person, who interjects numerous objections, quick to accuse bias or racism, and constantly threatens to appeal any ruling not found in her favor. She is a disgrace to our profession. Thank you for yielding the time to me Judge Henderson."

"Any other questions or comments?" Judge Henderson asked. Receiving none, he polled the judges.

First, he called for a verdict on defendant Daniel Blackstone. The verdict was unanimous: guilty, a Level One Sentence.

Next, he polled the eight judges for a finding on Summer Tillson and received, with his vote, a verdict of guilty: a Level One Sentence.

"Sergeant-of-arms, please notify the SDL of the court's decision and request for immediate execution of sentence. Striking the gavel he said, "This court is adjourned."

CHAPTER 24

Agent Wilson asked Jeannie, "Did you hear about that scumbag Beaumont?" He started to choke due to talking too fast and had to pause.

"Yeah, I heard it on the news--that he and two others were found dead in his mountain top retreat. When I heard it, I thought that it couldn't happen to a nicer asshole," she replied.

"No, I mean, yes; but, I heard from a friend of mine in the NSA that the three of them were killed by a drone crashing into the mansion carrying VX gas."

"Jesus, VX gas! Who were the other two inside?" Jeannie asked.

"His wife and eldest son. I can't remember their names," he responded.

"VX gas! How would someone get access to that?" asked Flores. "The first time I heard about that shit was in that Sean Connery movie, *The Rock*. I Googled it and man, that stuff kills you within seconds. If the movie was accurate, those sons-of-a-bitches died a horrible death."

Jeannie remembered her thoughts and the outspoken words she said to her television set when she first heard the news, requesting that it would be nice if his wife and son were the other two killed. Come on God, I was only teasing.

A surveillance team had been watching Judge Baldwin's home for several hours, but did not see any activity. Upon Jeannie and her team's arrival, they advised her, and left. Jeannie thanked them while exiting her vehicle. Flores, Jeannie, and Wilson took the front door and would announce to Judge Baldwin upon his answering the door, that they had a search warrant. Burk and the other two agents were assigned the duty of watching the back door with little expectation the Judge would quickly try to flee.

Flores knocked on the door several times, getting no answer. Jeannie told them to kick the door in, and the door was breached. Flores, Jeannie, and Wilson entered with Flores shouting, "FBI, we have a search warrant for the residence." Still no answer.

With their weapons drawn, they searched the residence and found it empty.

The house was the typical brownstone found in this part of the city with three large bedrooms, two baths, a moderate-sized kitchen, but a very small backyard. Skipping the kitchen, they made a cursory visual search of the three bedrooms. A spare bedroom had been converted into a study. Various law books decorated a built-in bookcase. There, on the table, was a Dell computer with the lid shut.

"Well, here's one computer. Get Burk in here," Jeannie told Flores. Burk entered the room and said, "Alright," while sitting down at the desk. He opened the Dell's lid and shouted, "Hello there, what do we have here?" Jeannie and Flores looked over Burk's shoulder to a screen filled with young girls and boys posing nude. He scrolled to the next set of photos displaying many of these same young children engaged in sexual acts with adults. "Got the bastard," Jeannie said, patting Burk on the back.

Jeannie examined a calendar on a desk. "Shit, the judge is already on the sex island with Cartwright. He left last night." After advising her team of the judge's itinerary, she instructed them to continue their search.

"OK, everyone. We found a treasure trove of child porn on one computer. Let's do a thorough search, and I mean every drawer, book, shelf, everything. Bag it and tag it. Have we found his cellphone, or did he take it with him?" Agent Wilson raised his hand holding an iPhone. "Don't know if it's his, but I did find a phone," Wilson said.

"Good. Burk, once we get back to the office, take all of his electronic equipment down to the lab, but make sure you work with Darcy. I know the two of you will do a more complete job than anyone else down there."

"Will do," replied Burk. "Jeannie, he has several encrypted files on his desktop. Unless we get lucky and can guess this pervert's passwords, it's going to take some time."

"Do the best you and Darcy can," she said as she worked her way around the room, supervising the search.

CHAPTER 25

H e received a text in code, requesting that he check his email. He climbed back onto his soft-tail Harley and headed to his apartment. Ever cautious of being stopped by the cops, since many judge all Harley drivers as outlaw motorcyclists, he took his time getting home. Thoughts of who his next victim might be ran through his brain. Hey, what the hell, male, female, black, white, Asian. It didn't matter to him. The pay is what mattered, and the pay was good.

He first stopped at a corner liquor store and picked up a six-pack of Budweiser beer, and a small bag of BBQ potato chips. He liked to munch while reading his orders. Jessie, his longtime friend now living in Alaska, introduced him to the SDL about one-year ago. Never hearing of the group before Jessie, he learned that the abbreviation stood for Sons and Daughters of Liberty. Jessie told him it was a secret organization modeled after the Sons of Liberty before and during the American Revolution. He would learn what they did much later from Jessie.

Cool, he thought. He remembered loving U.S. history in school and could still recall watching the old Disney movie, Johnny Tremain, in class. His teacher said it was an old movie, kind of corny, but even so it displayed the patriotism and risks these young Americans faced during that period of our nation's history. He loved the song when the Sons of Liberty marched to light up the Liberty Tree. *"We are the sons, yes we are the sons, the Sons of Liberty."*

Arriving home, he checked the neighborhood for suspicious vehicles. The FBI and CIA could be anywhere, he thought. Paranoid? Sure, in this society you had to be. There were too many people wanting to destroy his country, but not if he could do something about it. This attitude was why Jessie eventually told him about the SDL group and the opportunity to make some serious coin.

He put the six-pack on the kitchen counter and removed one of the bottles. Popping the cap, he grabbed the bag of chips and walked into a second bedroom dedicated as a study. He went to the bedroom window and closed the drapes. Opening his Mac Pro, he opened his encrypted server and found several received emails. One immediately caught his eye. The email was sent from SDL and upon opening it, saw that he was to make a pick up at a video game room inside the local Regal theaters. No other instructions were given, but he knew the drill by now. This was his third assignment.

Gee, the new *John Wick* film's out. I think I'll take in the movie after I grab the thumb drive, he thought. He found the video game machine and after making sure he was not being watched by anyone, including the two teenagers playing games about eight-feet way, he reached to the rear of the machine and found the taped drive. He quickly removed the drive and placed it in his left front Levi jeans' pocket. He then bought a bag of popcorn, a medium-sized Dr. Pepper, grabbed some napkins and proceeded to the proper theater.

Making sure he was not being followed, he arrived home and secured his Harley. Retracing his steps from earlier, he was once again back in his second bedroom inserting the thumb drive into the Mac. An encrypted PowerPoint file was the only item on his screen. He clicked on the icon and the first slide showed in large blue lettering, SDL. Advancing to the next slide, he saw a young white male displaying a ponytail and a red bandana tied across his forehead. Looks like a punk, he thought.

The next slide was split, showing the same individual on the left, with text on the right. "This individual is Daniel Blackstone. A confirmed anarchist, he's responsible for the death and mayhem of several individuals in both California and Oregon. He's been found guilty with a Level One Sentence." He continued to the next slide.

"This individual is attorney Summer Tillson. Another confirmed anarchist, she is the go- between from the financier to Blackstone. She relays orders to Blackstone and provides him with the cash to carry out his riots. She's been found guilty with a Level One Sentence. Execution of the sentences for both must be carried out within seven days."

Wow, a twofer. Serious money coming my way, he thought.

CHAPTER 26

hen the residence search was concluded, Jeannie and Agent Flores decided to head home. Burk had left earlier to meet Darcy at the lab. There was a steady drizzle coming down, making the roads slick, and realizing she had not had dinner, Jeannie decided to stop at an Applebee's. Initially, she was going for takeout, but decided one cocktail wouldn't hurt. After all, she and her team just took a pervert out of action, or he would be when he landed back in the states. Time to celebrate.

She could not interpret the red and white flashes that tried to invade her closed eyelids. Before she opened them, she felt the body lying next to her move ever so slightly. She opened her eyes and realized that the red and white flashes were coming from a motel sign outside the room she found herself in, advertising vacancies. How the hell did she get there, she asked herself, knowing she had blacked out again. She did not turn to see who was next to her. Instead, she slowly slide out of the bed and gathered up her clothing which appeared to have been dropped in a straight line from the motel room door to the bed. She started to cry as she quietly closed the door and left, not wanting to know who shared the room. This has to stop, she said to herself.

CHAPTER 27

ho was behind the SDL? Who are the members
of The Sons and Daughter of Liberty? And, for
that matter, was it a person or agency like the
FBI, NSA, or CIA that had the bucks he received for
his activities? He anticipated that someday they would
turn on him. Maybe not now; but yes, someday they
would consider him a liability and he would have to
be eliminated. For these reasons he never destroyed
any of the thumb drives or communication he
received. He needed some type of insurance policy
and with those pieces of evidence; he could always
blackmail them and keep himself from being killed.
Of course, if some sniper someday took his head off,
no one would learn about their existence, nor the part
he played with the SLD. Bummer, he thought.

This morning, he went to the Bank of America near
his home, and after gaining access to his safe deposit
box, he added the new thumb drive to his collection.
Inside the box was a detailed outline of all the targets
he had been assigned, and how he had carried out

their sentencing. There were separate receipts showing deposits he had received upon completion of each assignment. He included his latest assignment: that of Blackstone and Tillson and his initial plans for carrying out their sentences.

SDL informed him that Blackstone and Tillson always met at a local coffee shop, and that he would be notified when they were supposed to meet again. Why not take them out there, he thought? Sure, there might be some collateral damage, depending on the method he chose; but, didn't that happen in our country's war for independence? He needed to scout the joint out tonight so that he would be ready the moment he was provided with the date and time.

If they decided to drink their coffee as usual at an outside table near the sidewalk, he should be able to carry out the method he had chosen. The key was to find a parking spot close enough so that he could see their arrival and where they decided to sit. Piece of cake, he thought.

CHAPTER 28

J eannie was looking at a magazine in the waiting area of Medical Station #3 while waiting for her appointment with Dr. Marrow. She pretty much accepted that the doctor would confirm her pregnancy. How many months along was she? What would she do once it was verified by the doctor? What about work? How long could she conceal the fact? Not long, since Flores already guessed it. Shit, how did she fuck up her life so quickly?

"Jeannie Loomis," the same nursing assistant working during her previous visit announced.

Jeannie laid the magazine back on the table wondering how many germs were on the surface area, not to mention the pathogens being thrown around the waiting room from other patient's sneezing and coughing. Great place for an expectant woman to be sitting.

The nursing assistant took her vitals and discussed the nice weather outside. She did not ask Jeannie the purpose of her visit, nor did she even hint about the results of the pregnancy test. "The doctor will be in shortly," she said as she left the examining room.

Surprisingly, only a few minutes passed before Dr. Morrow entered. "Hello again," she said.

Jeannie responded with, "Fine I guess."

Dr. Marrow smiled and after sitting on a round doctor's stool rolled over to where Jeannie was seated at the foot of a gurney. "Well, I wanted to tell you in person the results of your pregnancy and blood tests. You are pregnant, probably six weeks into the first trimester." The doctor paused as if to gage how the news affected Jeannie. "You don't seem surprised?" she asked.

"No," Jeannie responded. I pretty much realized that I was expecting.

"Well, in the first trimester you might experience any of the following. What a minute, I have a chart; oh, here it is." She held a chart close to Jeannie and read the following,

"Extreme fatigue

Tender, swollen breasts.

Nipples may protrude.

Nausea with or without throwing up (morning sickness),

Cravings or aversion to certain foods,

Mood swings,

Constipation,

Frequent urination,

Headaches,

Heartburn, and

Weight gain or loss.

Some of the changes you'll experience in your first trimester may cause you to revise your daily routine. You may need to go to bed earlier, or eat more frequent or smaller meals. Some women experience a lot of discomfort and others may not feel any at all." The doctor placed the chart down on her table and asked Jeannie if she had been experiencing any of those symptoms?"

Jeannie identified the symptoms she had or was experiencing, adding that recently she's felt a burning sensation while urinating. "Do you think I have a urinary track infection?" Jeannie asked.

"No, that's the other reason I scheduled you for a one-on-one appointment with me. Since you stated on your last visit you'd been sexually active and sometimes do not practice safe sex, I requested an STD panel. Fortunately, you do not have Aids. You do have what we call a co-infection of gonorrhea and chlamydia."

"Oh shit! And with the baby on the way," Jeannie said panicking.

Dr. Morrow placed her right hand on Jeannie's shoulder and said, "Both infections can be cured when treated with antibiotics, often in a single dose. But, I must tell you Jeannie, it appears you're living a very risky lifestyle; I mean, beyond being an FBI agent. Fortunately, I didn't have to inform you of a HIV diagnosis: Aids. I suspect that alcohol is somehow related to the lifestyle you're living. Am I correct, or way off base?"

Jeannie began to cry and soon the sobbing became uncontrollable. "Shit, there goes my hormones," she said.

"Yes, as I pointed out on the chart, you'll experience mood changes; but Jeannie, I really suggest you speak with someone, and try to evaluate your style of living, especially now that you're with child. We have some excellent mental health advisers on staff if you want me to make a referral."

Jeannie used a tissue she took out of her purse and wiped the tears away. "No, thank you. We have psychologists at the bureau. I can talk to one of them when I feel the need. Thank you though."

Dr. Morrow did not respond, but instead tried to establish eye contract with Jeannie. Being unable to do so, she simply said, "OK, but seriously, you need to seek help. You already have a highly stressful and dangerous job, and now your body is trying to adjust for a second person. Seeking help is not a sign of weakness."

"I understand doctor, and I really will see someone and get my act together." She put out her hand to thank Doctor Morrow who did the same. "Is there anything else I need to do today? Jeannie asked.

The doctor stood and said she will have her nursing assistant return with some pamphlets on what to expect during each trimester, and a prescription for some vitamins and supplementals for Jeannie to take. She also told her to stop at the injection center, Medical Station #7, so she can get the STD shot. With that, the doctor left.

CHAPTER 29

I'm a genius even if I say so myself, he thought as he got out of the shower. There will not be any collateral damage with this method, and the two targets will experience very painful deaths, payback for the pain and suffering they caused those elderly people who died in Portland or Berkeley, wherever. He got on the computer and sent an encrypted email to the SDL requesting a dropoff of a product needed for the execution of sentences on Tillson and Blackstone. He requested a text stating the time and date when he can meet the contact for pickup.

On his bed was the modified umbrella he modeled after the weapon used to kill Bulgarian dissident Georgi Markov while he waited for a bus near the Waterloo Bridge on September 7, 1978. Inserted into the main shaft of the umbrella was a standard BB-gun. The trigger mechanism was mounted near the handle. I bet someone in the SDL is wondering what the hell this stuff is besides the Ricin I'm ordering, he thought.

Amazingly, the next morning he found an encrypted response for SDL with instructions as to the time and place for pickup. He had just enough time to stop at an AM/PM store, gas up his hog, grab a bag of Hostess donuts and coffee, and make it to the ballpark. It looked like a good game between the San Francisco Giants, currently with the best winning percentage of all the majors, and the Central Division-leading Chicago Cubs. He went to the Will-call booth and asked for a ticket left in his name. The clerk gave him the ticket and he entered Oracle Stadium, stopping to get some garlic fries, a hotdog, and beer before searching for his seat.

Section 124, row 8, seat 1 were great seats along the third-base side near the Giants' dugout. He spotted some of his favorite players, and while watching them take batting practice, placed the hotdog, garlic fries and beer on the seat next to his. He casually reached under his seat with his right hand and found a package about the size of a double pack of gum taped to the bottom.

He pulled on the tape and freed the package. Not examining it, he quickly placed it in the inside pocket of his jacket. He ate his food and watched the game until the fifth inning, leaving with the Giants ahead 4 – 1.

When he got home, he turned his alarm system off, made sure the perimeter of his home was secure, closed all drapes, and placed the package on his kitchen counter near the sink. He had worked with Ricin before and was comfortable handling it. But, this new more deadly agent was a whole new ballgame for him.

Batrachotoxin, similar to Curare, comes from the skins of tiny frogs found in western Colombia. Native Indians in Western Colombia collect these frogs--golden *Phyllobates terribilis* and multicolored *Phyllobates*--and sweat out the poison over a fire before putting it on their darts. It only takes an amount the size of two grains of table salt to kill a person.

Batrachotoxin kills by interfering with sodium ion channels in the cells of muscles and nerves, jamming them open so they do not close. Ultimately the victim dies of heart failure.

He took an amount of both the Ricin and Batrachotoxin and placed them in a bowl. He then counted out several BBs and dropped them into the solution, covered the solution with a piece of Saran wrap, and placed it in his refrigerator. Now all he needed was the time of the meet between Blackstone and Tillson.

CHAPTER 30

I'm going to be a mother, Jeannie thought. She vacillated between panic and joy. While in the joy phase, she wondered if it was going to be a boy or girl, and if she would want to know via ultrasound or just be surprised at delivery. Panic brought on a lot of questions such as how could she handle her job during pregnancy, and who would care for her baby after birth? Both of her parents were gone and she had no brothers of sisters. The more she thought about it, the more she realized the FBI was pretty much her life. That thought brought on more thoughts about rumors and jokes being made at her expense. She could hear it now: "Hey, here comes the slut who chased after the Ark and came up empty. Well, she ain't empty now. She's got a bun in the oven."

And what about Dr. Marrow's comments? Did she indeed need professional help? she thought. Nah, everyone wakes up after blacking out from too much booze and finds themselves in bed with a stranger whom they just had sex with, right? "Please God, help me," she said out loud, surprising herself.

She was brought back to present time and space with the sound of her cellphone ringing. She glanced at the screen and saw it was Burk. "Hey, Burk. What do you have?"

"Well, Jeannie, we think we've only scratched the surface, but you really need to see what we've recovered so far. What time do you expect to be in tomorrow morning?"

"How long are you two going to be there tonight?" Jeannie responded.

"Probably for a few more hours. Besides the files that'll cook the judge's ass, we found some other files referring to something called the Star Chamber, and someone or something identified only by the letters 'SDL.'"

"Huh," Jeannie said. "I'll be there in fifteen to twenty minutes. Have you two eaten yet?"

"No, could you bring us something? That would be great."

"I'll order a pizza and pick it up on the way. What kind of soda do you each want?"

God, the pizza smelled so good she was tempted to stop and pull a piece out and eat it while driving. Her thoughts flashed to the chart the doctor showed her--increased appetite. Resisting the temptation, she arrived at the bureau and met with Burk and Darcy. Darcy was a slightly heavy Latina, but her outgoing personality made her an asset in a very stressful environment like the FBI. She was your stereotypical computer nerd who appeared to have no interest in the opposite sex, nor same sex--nor sex in general. Guys would make obvious attempts bordering on sexual harassment, but Darcy was clueless. But, what Jeannie liked about her, was her uncanny ability around computers, especially in breaking down firewalls, dissecting moving international servers used by criminals to hide their primary locations, and overcoming encrypted files. And boy, could see track-down hackers. The more complicated the issue, the more she got turned on.

"We could smell you coming," said Burk and Jeannie entering Darcy's office.

"Hi, Darcy. How are you?" Jeannie asked.

"Hi, Jeannie. I'm fine. Thank you for asking me to assist in the Judge Baldwin's case."

"Hey, when I want the best, I ask for the best. Let's eat, I'm starving." Jeannie replied.

Jeannie put away three large slices of pizza. Burk noticed and said, "Gee Jeannie, you really were hungry."

Jeannie, trying to cover the real reason for her appetite said, "Yeah, I was so busy today I didn't have time for lunch. OK, so what did you two find?"

"Well, do you want to see all of the child porn we found? Believe me, there are over 20,000 pictures of children as young as six-months involved," Burk said.

"No, you know what the prosecution needs, so you put that portion of the case together. Save everything on a CD and make two copies, one for the file and one for the charging department."

"Got it," Burk said. "Okay, Darcy, bring up that other stuff."

Darcy wheeled the mouse around with efficiency and brought up a file labeled Star Chamber.

"Star Chamber," Jeannie said. "Isn't that the old film with Michael Douglas and…shit, who else? Oh yeah, Hal Holbrook?"

Darcy looked at Burk, and Burk turned and looked at Jeannie with a quizzical look on his face.

"God, I forgot you two are babies. Star Chamber was a great movie starring Douglas and Holbrook who were judges. They, and other judges met in secret to review cases where defendants got off on technicalities. They tried these individuals in absentia. If the defendants were found guilty, they were killed."

Neither Burk nor Darcy spoke, instead continuing to look at Jeannie. Darcy, feeling a little embarrassed, grabbed her soda and sipped some of her Mountain Dew. Frustrated, Jeannie grabbed her cellphone and started reading, "Star Chamber, a film made in 1983 starring Michael Douglas as a naïve judge becoming increasingly frustrated with criminals avoiding punishment due to flaws in the law." Darcy and Burk were still clueless.

"OK, never mind. Show me what's in the file."

CHAPTER 31

The text read: "meeting tomorrow, 10:00 a.m." He deleted the text, went into the kitchen and opened the refrigerator door. He looked at the covered bowl and swished the BBs around in the solution. He grabbed an egg and scrambled it. He cooked a sausage patty, some hash browns, and put a slice of wheat bread in the toaster. As he was preparing his breakfast, he tried to visualize how things would happen tomorrow morning at the coffee shop.

He took his breakfast plate to the study and opened up his computer. He began typing a detailed outline of his plan for tomorrow. After finishing up both his breakfast and the document, he printed it out and checked his watch to see if the bank was open. It was, so he placed the empty plate in the sink, folded the paper and placed it in his shirt pocket, grabbed his helmet and went out the door making sure he set his alarm.

He got up at 6 a.m. the next morning, wanting to be the first in line at the rental company when they opened. He had called them when he got back from placing his latest document in his safety deposit box, confirming that they had a van he could rent. He had no intention of returning the van; he would dump it somewhere after he carried out his mission.

He had an Uber driver drop him off at the rental company. The van had exactly what he was looking for: dark side plexiglass windows. Using false identification and a stolen credit card, he secured the vehicle and drove back to his residence and entered the garage. He entered his home and checked his watch. 7:30 a.m., plenty of time to catch some news and have another cup of coffee.

At 8:30 he got the modified umbrella containing the guts of a BB gun and opened the slot to load the BBs. He placed the umbrella on the kitchen counter using several kitchen towels to keep the gun in an upside-down position, making it easier to insert the BBs. He removed the bowl from the refrigerator and grabbed a pair of tweezers. Taking one BB at a time, he slowing placed it in the barrel of the gun. It was probably overkill to load the gun with ten BBs, but he wanted to be on the safe side just in case he missed his targets.

He covered the solution still in the bowl with plastic wrap, slowly walked to the bathroom and peeled back the wrap, and poured the liquid into the toilet which he then flushed. He rinsed the bowl in the sink using plastic gloves and then placed it in his dishwasher, selecting the timer for a forty-five-minute cleaning cycle. He doubted that the assassin who killed the Bulgarian dissident Georgi Markov was as slick as he was, especially if he could take down both targets instead of just one.

It was now 9a.m., time to head to the coffee shop and find a good parking space where he could view the arrival of Blackstone and Tillson. There was a fine mist falling. Perfect, a person with an umbrella would not cause suspicion. Finding a parking space almost immediately, he decided to visit the coffee shop and get a cup. The banana bread looked good, so he ordered a slice. He took the coffee and banana bread back to the van and moved to the interior next to one of the side windows where he had placed a folding chair. Now he just had to wait for them to show up.

He was not disappointed. The first to arrive was Tillson. She did look like a throwback to the radicals of the 1960s, wearing a colorful blouse covered by a rawhide-like vest. Her hair was made up in what he thought might be dreadlocks, normally sported by Blacks. Torn knee jeans and black combat boots completed her ensemble. She entered the coffee shop and returned with a cup of hot water and a few tea bags which she began dunking into the water.

Blackstone showed up five minutes late. He first walked up and said something to Tillson, laughed and entered the coffee shop, returning with a large cup of what seemed to be coffee. Should have tried the banana bread, asshole, the assassin thought.

OK, the targets are seated, time to roll. He cocked the modified BB gun with sound suppressor that was inserted into the shaft of the umbrella. He waited until no one was walking to the curbside of the van and exited. The mist was so fine it would not seem necessary for anyone to open an umbrella, but this was even better because his aim would not be constricted by the fabric of the parasol.

Walking towards the two sitting under a covering from the rain, Blackstone was the closest. He slightly raised the umbrella to the calf area of Blackstone's right leg. He pulled the trigger. The BB gun that he modified had more than enough power to break through the cloth fabric of Blackstone's pants. Blackstone quickly put his hand on the calf area while still in conversation with Tillson. He rubbed it hard a few times, but then returned to placing his hand on his cup of coffee.

The assassin continued his short walk away from the two and when clear, cocked the next BB into the chamber. He made a turn, retracing his trip. Tillson was sipping her tea while watching Blackstone rub his leg again. From a short distance, the assassin fired at Tillson's left calf. Her reaction was similar to Blackstone. Two shots, two hits. The suppressor and the sound of the coffee drinkers eliminated any sound for the BB gun action. Mission complete.

He walked across the street and entered the van. When it was clear, he returned to his stool and began looking out the window, waiting for the inevitable to occur. Surprisingly, Tillson was the first to show signs of distress. The assassin knew the signs of Ricin exposure, but this was the first time he had used batrachotoxin. He knew that death was unavoidable, but had only read about signs leading up to death. Now he was going to be able to witness it first-hand.

Tillson began having uncontrollable convulsions. She grabbed for her throat as if she were suffocating. Blackstone began showing the same reactions almost as if he were mimicking Tillson. It appeared that several other patrons witnessing the event thought it was an act, laughing, and one person actually applauding. Blackstone fell off his chair and was laying on his side twitching. Tillson simply appeared to have passed out and fell into her cup of tea, sending spray from their table. Her vomit and blood covered the tabletop. In less than 10 minutes, long before an ambulance appeared, they were both dead. He knew, however, that even if paramedics had arrived sooner, there is no effective antidote for batrachotoxin poisoning. He put the van in gear and was leaving his parking space when the van's tires squealed a little due to the rain.

CHAPTER 32

66 **T**here are several references to someone or
something identified with the letters SDL.
I ran it through several search engines, but
have not found a match," Darcy said.

"Keep looking. There has to be some type of
connection between the Star Chamber and SDL. I
think you should focus on what Star Chamber is since
Baldwin was a sitting judge, so it must be related to
some type of court or tribunal, something like that.
There's something there and I just can't put my finger
on it," Jeannie said.

Jeannie left Darcy and Burk, telling them she was
going home and would see them in the morning.
She felt her stomach which was weird, since nothing
was stirring yet. This thought brought a smile to her
face—she was going to be a mom.

There was an intense desire to stop at a bar on the
way home for a quick one, but Jeannie had made a
commitment to herself and her baby, that it was time
to clean up her act. Instead, she stopped at a small

family-owned Chinese restaurant and ordered some pork chow mein with pan-fried noodles. She thought that was a healthy choice but realized that once the Judge Baldwin matter was wrapped up, she needed a more disciplined change in her lifestyle. That included a gym membership.

The next morning after taking her shower, Jeannie examined her nude body in the long mirror hanging from the inside of her bathroom door. Not showing yet, she folded up her bath towel and after putting on a blouse, put the towel under the garment trying to envision what she would look like in a few months. Speaking out loud she said, "Ok, little guy or girl, we are in this together."

She found the loosest fitting, yet still figure-showing pair of pants and put them on. Making mental notes that she needed to start buying maturity clothes, yet thought about how, realistically, she could hide her pregnancy. Then Jeannie remembered that she had forgotten to contact Agent Delaney at Interpol about Michael Cartwright, his sex-trafficking and sex island case. She would call him once she got to her office.

She boiled an egg and toasted a bagel while warming up some water for tea. She turned on Fox News to see what was happening in the world.

"Known activist attorney, Summer Tillson, and an un-named white male died today at a local coffee shop in downtown Seattle. Police have not provided any additional information, but other patrons sitting

near the two individuals say that it appeared both were chocking before they collapsed. A coroner assistant, as well as a hazmat team can be seen here collecting the cups and left-over liquids, placing them in hazmat bags. The coffee shop has closed at the request of the police. We will continue to monitor this developing situation and provide updates as we receive them."

"Huh," Jeannie thought, as she remembered what her late father had said numerous times: that celebrities, whether it be actors, politicians, or sports figures, all seem to die in triplets. First, the former Secretary of State McKenzie died from a fall. Next, Beaumont was killed in his home with his son and umpteenth wife. Now, Tillson and an unknown male died outside a coffee shop in Seattle. Sure seems strange.

She arrived at the bureau before Flores or Burk. Of course, she did not expect Burk to be in this early. She could only speculate how long he and Darcy worked on Judge Baldwin's computer last night. "Can't wait to see if they found anything else in their search," she thought to herself.

CHAPTER 33

J eannie's desk phone rang. It was Davenport's secretary, Stephanie. "Hi Stephanie, how's it going?" Jeannie said upon answering.

"Don't ask," Stephanie said.

"That bad, huh?" Jeannie responded.

"Yeah, some afternoon I'd love to meet with you since I'm not sure what I need to do," Stephanie said.

"Just let me know the place and time, and I'll be there," replied Jeannie. "What's up?"

"The SAC needs to see you asap. What about? I have no clue," Stephanie said.

"OK, I'm on my way," came Jeannie's response. "See you soon."

While leaving her office she ran into Flores and Burk walking down the hallway together.

"Hey, Jeannie, you will not believe what we found on the computer," said Burk.

"Can't wait to see it, but I've been summoned by the SAC, so it'll have to wait. I'll check in when I get back. By the way, one of you needs to remind me when

I get back from his highness, to call Interpol so I can give Agent Delaney the info we have on Cartwright." With that, Jeannie headed towards Davenport's office.

"Loomis, I assume you heard about that incident in Seattle involving Tillson," Davenport inquired before Jeannie took a seat opposite him.

"Just what I heard this morning on the news," she replied.

"The locals seem to have most of it under control, but administration wants an FBI presence because of Tillson's standing in the community; so, get up there as soon as possible and offer assistance."

"But sir, we're still wrapping up the case against Judge Baldwin. Is it really necessary that I go up there?" Jeannie inquired.

"Yes, I feel it is necessary. Your team should be able to complete the investigation.--hopefully to a more successful conclusion that your prior case."

"You fucker!" Jeannie thought. "How long do you want me to be in Seattle?" she asked.

"I'll leave that up to your discretion, but do enough so we can tell the press that FBI assistance was offered and accepted," was Davenport's response. With that, she was dismissed.

In the outer office Stephanie asked if Jeannie was free to meet at a local pub located a few blocks from the bureau. Jeannie said that she had just been ordered to fly up to Seattle on the Tillson death investigation, but that she hoped to be back in two days. Once back, she would notify Stephanie and meet.

Back at her desk, she called Interpol and reached Agent Delaney.

"Agent Loomis, how are you?" he asked upon answering his phone.

"Fine, and you?" she replied.

"How do you say it in America, another day, another Euro?" he said while laughing.

"Something like that," Jeannie said. "The reason I'm calling is that during our investigation into a judge heavily into child pornography, we found evidence linked to Michael Cartwright."

"Cartwright," Agent Delaney said. "We've tried many times to make a case against him, but we never had enough hard evidence to go forward. I'm very interested to hear what you have on him."

She told him about the wiretap, the child porn found on Judge Baldwin's computer, the child sex trafficking, and especially the sex island destination. Delaney wrote down the information as quickly as Jeannie gave him the details. When she finished, Delaney said, "Agent Loomis, you have provided more than enough evidence for Interpol to proceed. I will contact you once we have concluded our investigation. Thank you so much."

"One more thing I would like to discuss with you, Agent Delaney, if you have the time," Jeannie said.

"Of course, of course. With this latest information about Cartwright, how can I not pay you back?" Delaney said. "What do you need?" he added.

"Just out of curiosity, what can you tell me about the death of Beaumont, his son, and wife?"

There was a short period of silence but before Jeannie asked if Delaney was still on the line, and then he said, "Agent Loomis, could I please have your cellphone number?"

Jeannie gave it to him and he told her to expect a call soon from an unlisted number.

Her cell rang and she could tell the caller id was blocked. "This is Loomis," she said.

"Agent Loomis, what I am about to tell you is extremely sensitive and highly confidential,"

Delaney said. "I understand," Jeannie responded. Delaney continued, "Beaumont, as you are aware, was killed by VX gas. The delivery method was through the use of a drone. The killer maneuvered the drone directly to the bedroom areas of the house and then crashed the drone into the interior. Your CIA and NSA are involved with both our agency and the Swiss authorities, but to date, they have not made much progress as to who was responsible."

"Thank you, Agent Delaney. Good luck on your investigation into Cartwright," Jeannie said, and with that they both terminated the phone call. Jeannie had not learned much more from Delaney, but the thoughts of her father kept creeping into her mind: they always die in threes.

CHAPTER 34

Jeannie met up with Flores, Burk, and Darcy. She told them of her meeting with the SAC and that she would be flying out that afternoon to Seattle. Flores let his feelings known about Davenport sending Jeannie to Washington, especially the liberal city of Seattle. He also knew that Jeannie would not be received with open arms by the local cops who always seemed to feel that the big, bad, FBI would swoop in and take credit anytime a case was solved.

Jeannie, attempting to calm Flores down, diverted her attention from Flores to Darcy and Burk. "OK, tell me the magic you two share; find us a bunch of new evidence to put Baldwin away for a very long time."

"What we found," Burk said, "are dates in which this Star Chamber met. No hard information, but it seems to fit that the Star Chamber is some type of court as you guessed. There's a related encrypted file that we're still trying to gain access to; we think it might supplement the information we have about what goes on in this Star Chamber, as well as what SDL stands for."

"Also, we found two prominent names, but not with references to Star Chamber or SDL. Those are Beaumont and McKenzie," Darcey said with a big smile on her face.

"Holy shit!" said Jeannie. "Beaumont and McKenzie?"

"Yup! Some kind of coincidence, huh?" Darcy said.

"Jeannie doesn't believe in coincidences," said Flores. Jeannie just smiled without comment.

"Alright. Good work. Keep digging and keep all of this confined to this room until we can sort it out. I hope to make my appearance in Seattle short and sweet, and be back in two days. If you find anything else, reach me by cell." With this, Jeannie returned to her office, picked up her purse and left.

CHAPTER 35

The van was hit broadside while the assassin was leaving the scene of his latest triumph. Self-congratulating thoughts prevented him from seeing a vehicle fail to stop for a red light, crashing into the driver's side of the van. He never knew what hit him.

Paramedics pulled him from the mangled van where the airbag failed to explode and the door post broke his neck, before his face impacted with the windshield, creating an intricate spider web design; although, he never had time to admire it.

When he was pulled from the van he flatlined. It was only through numerous compressions by the paramedic that his heart-beat returned. Upon arrival at the hospital, the doctors quickly diagnosed several broken ribs, one of which had penetrated the heart, in addition to a broken neck. The doctors surmised he was not wearing a seatbelt. He was rushed to surgery with a 50-50 chance of survival.

Jeannie arrived at the Sea-Tac Airport at 9 a.m., opting for an early flight in hopes of wrapping things up from an FBI perceptive, so she could return the next day. Having carryon luggage allowed her to quickly exit the airport where she found an awaiting Seattle police vehicle with driver at curbside in a Police Only area.

"Agent Loomis? I'm officer Stewart. I'm supposed to take you to either your hotel room or the station. It's up to you."

"I only have this carryon, so let's go to your station so I can get up to speed," Jeannie responded.

Upon arrival, she was introduced to Detective Sergeant Hardin. A twenty-five-year veteran of the force, she expected him to treat her with professionalism, yet have a bad taste in his mouth about intervention from the FBI. Sporting male-pattern baldness and a 1980s mustache, he was still in excellent shape.

Instead, she was pleasantly surprised by his demeanor. He offered her coffee which she accepted since they had decaf, thinking of her baby. Detective Hardin told her there had been a major development while she was in the air.

"Really, what happened?" Jeannie asked.

He started by telling her in chronological order how the first call came in. Knowing that Jeannie obviously knew one of the victims was Summer Tillson, he told her the identity of the male.

"Guy's name is Daniel Blackstone," Hardin said.

"Daniel Blackstone? Known anarchist?" Jeannie said.

"One and the same," Hardin said with the hint of a small smile.

"Wow! We have the famous anti-everything American Summer Tillson meeting with the infamous anarchist Daniel Blackstone. Wonder what they were planning?" Jeannie stated with a small smile on her face.

"Is that the big break I missed while 30,000 feet in the sky?" She asked.

"No, I was saving the best part for last," said Hardin. "Let's take a ride," he said, noticing that Jeannie had finished her cup of coffee.

Jeannie asked if she could leave her carryon at Hardin's desk. He said sure and grabbed her bag and placed it under his desk. He looked at an unidentified detective and said he was heading out to the evidence garage, and to notify him if anything came from the hospital.

While walking out to his gray-colored Dodge Charger, he continued to bring Jeannie up to date. "While the two victims were struggling for their lives, a van was seen leaving a parking space across from the coffee shop. Most people probably would never take notice of a car leaving, but fortunately, one of our off-duty patrol officers happened to be walking towards that location when one of the victims,

Blackstone, fell to the ground. While everyone else watched, two sickos actually began taking pictures on their cellphones. Our officer heard squeals from a van making a U-turn and drive away. He wrote down the plate ID, but it didn't matter since later it was determined to be stolen, and the van had already been involved in a traffic accident.

"I can hardly wait for the finale," Jeannie said.

"Oh, it has a happy ending," Hardin said.

"Do tell," she replied.

"The driver of the van was T-boned at an intersection about two blocks away from the coffee shop. Never saw what hit him. Unfortunately for him, an ambulance, already directed to the scene at the coffee shop, continued on and didn't stop to help him. By the time a second ambulance arrived at the accident, the paramedics found him unconscious and bleeding. Fire crew got him out of the van and his heart stopped. Paramedic brought him back, but he was unconscious and is in really bad shape. Doctors don't know if he's going to make it."

"Well gee, I thought you said this had a happy ending," Jeannie said.

Before Hardin responded, they arrived at a large garage with a sign saying Seattle Police Department-- Only Authorized Personnel.

They both got out and walked to the rollup door. Hardin punched in a code and the door began to rise. Jeannie saw numerous cars, motorcycles, and a few vans parked across from each other with a space of approximately 30 foot between the two opposing rows, which allowed people to walk the distance of the warehouse if they desired.

Hardin walked up to a van showing signs of major impact.

"This guy is lucky he's still alive," Jeannie said.

"Yup! Always seems that the assholes survive a crash, but innocent people don't," said Hardin. He went to the side door and opened it. It was opposite the driver's side of the van and had the least damage.

Jeannie noticed that the only thing in the van was what appeared to be a folding chair, now laying on its side. "You're showing me this for a reason, right?" Jeannie said.

Without saying anything, Hardin climbed into the van, leaving Jeannie to observe from the sliding van door. Hardin unfolded the chair and placed it as near as he could to the smashed side window. "OK, here's what we believe happened to the bad guy who's in the hospital in a coma. By the way, we found no identification on him, and since he's out of it, we're awaiting the results of his prints to find out his true identity. We ran the van's VIN and found that the van was rented here in the city, but all the paperwork this guy provided is false."

Hardin turned and faced the side window. "This guy finds a parking space across from the coffee shop, directly across from the area the two victims meet up and are drinking their brew. He decides the time is right, gets out of the van and cuts across the street carrying an umbrella."

"An umbrella? What did he do, smack them over the head and cause them to choke to death?" Jeannie asked, knowing that was not the case but trying to inject a little humor into the story.

"Yeah, the old umbrella over-the-head maneuver. You FBI agents never heard about that?" he asked while laughing. "Anyway, he does the dirty and gets back in the van and starts to make his get-away when bam, he becomes lunchmeat in a van sandwich."

"OK, tell me about the umbrella," Jeannie said, smiling at the lunchmeat metaphor.

"When our patrol units arrived at the traffic accident, one of the officers decided to look in the van to confirm what the paramedic had already determined: no other occupants. He opened the rear door and saw next to the folding chair what appeared to be an umbrella. He was about ready to close the van door when he noticed what appeared to be a trigger mechanism on its shaft. He grabbed the umbrella and heard something rattle like BBs in a BB gun. He continued to exam the umbrella and confirmed that it was a trigger device. He placed it back where he found it and decided that with what occurred down the street at the coffee shop, the two might be related. He told his sergeant who requested yours truly to respond."

"Well, detective, we at the FBI are impressed. Outstanding police work," Jeannie said, having a hard time resisting a hardy laugh.

Hardin, who had now exited the van, bent over as if taking a bow. "Thank you, thank you," he said. "Now, the most interesting part" he continued.

"You mean there's even more?" Jeannie joked.

"After photographing the umbrella, I took it from the van and heard the sound of BBs rolling back and forth. Thank God I didn't open the shaft to confirm that the rattling was coming from BBs or something else. Instead, I heard a caution warning coming across the radio of a patrol officer standing next to me. The caution was from the coroner's assistant who, as it turned out, had served two terms overseas with the army fighting Sadam. You know, those whole weapons of mass destruction stuff? Well, that was his assignment in the Army: to help identify and decontaminate soldiers exposed to that stuff. Anyway, the warning was that the two victims appeared to have been exposed to Ricin and everyone was told to watch what they touched, and so on."

"Jesus," Jeannie said. "You mean, the bad guy loaded the rifle, or whatever, with BBs laced with Ricin and shot the two victims?"

"Worse. Because the coroner's assistant quickly suspected Ricin as having caused the deaths of the two victims, he rushed a "tox" screen because he had never heard of Ricin working this fast. As it turned out, he was right. Ever heard of Batrachotoxin?"

"No," Jeannie said. "Bad stuff?"

"Major bad. Comes from the skin of a certain type of frog in Colombia or someplace. Once this stuff gets into your system, Sayonara baby. Dead in less than ten minutes. When we finally had a hazmat team open the cylinder, we found eight other BBs laced with both Ricin and Batrachotoxin."

They returned to the station where Jeannie picked up her carryon luggage and Hardin dropped her off at the Four Seasons where she checked in, and after ordering room service took a hot shower. She checked her cellphone and found several texts. One was from Burk, the other from Agent Delaney of Interpol. Checking her watch and accounting for the time difference, she decided to call Delaney when she woke up in the morning. She called Burk.

He answered his phone on the second ring and asked how Seattle was?

"Cold, damp and foggy. What else is new?" she told him. "How's the computer search going?"

"I think we hit the jackpot. Darcy and I were finally able to get into most of his files, and we now know that the Star Chamber is a secret court, something like the one in that movie you talked about. The letters SDL stands for the Sons and Daughters of Liberty. Mind you, we still haven't connected all the dots, but the puzzle is slowly coming together."

"Who or what are the Sons and Daughters of Liberty," Jeannie asked.

"It appears that the Star Chamber, the court, meets somewhere. A trial takes place and the sentence is sent to the SDL for execution. We're hoping that the last remaining files, if we can crack them, will give us the final pieces like the whereabouts of the Star Chamber, members, SDL info, and so on."

"OK, keep on it. I'd planned on returning this afternoon, but there are a lot of loose ends up here, so I won't be heading back until tomorrow," Jeannie said.

CHAPTER 36

"**G**entlemen, please be seated," Judge Roberts requested while striking the gavel on the base. "As you are aware, unfortunately, Judge Baldwin has been taken into police custody. The charges he's accused of committing are extremely serious, and I feel it's safe to say he will be facing a long prison incarceration. Our sources tell us he's remained silent, so for the present moment the Star Chamber is safe. I've called each of you here for this emergency session since we must do everything in our power to protect this body. As I stated in my phone conversations with you, I believe that if planned properly by the SDL, we can make sure this body can continue its much-needed work. Each of you knows the targets, and because of the scale, if you agree, SDL will be authorized to use whatever means necessary. I'll now poll the court."

"Judge Swartz?"
"Aye."

"Judge Kalford?"
"Aye."
"Judge Hall?"
"Aye."
"Judge Silverman?"
"Aye."
"Judge Henderson?"
"Aye."
"Judge Kanamoto?"
"Aye."
"Judge Kavanaugh?*"*
"Aye."
"I vote aye, making the vote unanimous. Sergeant-of-arms, please inform the SDL of our decision. This court is adjourned." Judge Roberts struck the gavel and left his seat followed by the other judges.

CHAPTER 37

J eannie tried to fall asleep, but could not turn her mind off. She rolled out of bed and opened her carryon luggage and pulled out her notebook. She moved several objects from the hotel bedroom desk and made a large circle in the middle of the paper where she wrote, Star Chamber.

She then drew a line to the right connecting that circle to a new one. This one was labeled SDL and she placed a small question mark next to it. Working her way around the larger middle circle she added several other circles containing McKenzie, Beaumont, Judge Baldwin, Blackstone, and Tillson. She then stood up and peered down at her drawings. "There's something there," she thought, "but I just can't see it."

Checking the time, she made a call to Agent Delaney. His secretary answered, and she transferred the call to his phone.

"Agent Loomis, great timing. I was about to call you with the good news," he said in a rapid, excited voice. "Your information paid off. We caught Cartwright with thirteen teenage males and females, some as young as ten-years-old. I don't want to discuss the names of these individuals on the phone but suffice to say, we did catch a few politicians, sports figures, and some Hollywood elites in various sexual acts with these minors. Also, we found Cartwright's computer before he could shut it off, and found names going back seven years, citing dates and times of their visits, and their sexual pleasures. Your Judge Baldwin has visited the island many times."

"Agent Delaney, it's extremely important that you try and contain information from the media about the raid, and especially the names of individuals you arrested. I believe there's a connection between Cartwright, the island, and some recent deaths of high profile individuals here and abroad. Have you heard about the Deep State here in our government?" she asked.

"Yes, I am aware of this Deep State. Perhaps we should talk later when it is safe to do so. I will do everything in my power to keep the details of the raid confidential and on a need-to-know basis. For how long, I do not know. Two of the individuals captured in the raid are U.S. Congressmen. They are already requesting that the American Embassy be contacted so they can return to the United States. I will delay this from happening as long as I can. I think that if they return to U.S. soil, your Deep State will attempt to erase this from ever getting out."

"Thank you. I promise to get back to you as soon as possible once I tie everything together. Talk to you soon." With this, Jeannie hung up.

Detective Hardin picked Jeannie up at the hotel. He had a cup of decaf coffee for her, and offered some cream and sweetener. While putting both in her cup, she was told they got a hit on the assassin's name. James Burgess, a twenty-three year old loner, last known residence--right there in Seattle. No criminal record other than a traffic violation. He was still in a coma, but they were able to secure a search warrant for his residence, and that was their destination.

Burgess's home was a non-descript ranch style home in a middle-calls subdivision. The exterior of the house was well maintained: lawn cut, shrubs pruned. Nothing spectacular and nothing to earn anyone's attention. Before entering, they had the bomb disposal unit check out the exterior of the home, making sure the doors and windows were not boobytrapped. They then forced the front door open and entered. The alarm system activated, but one of the bomb disposal officers quickly deactivated it. After getting an all-clear from the bomb disposal sergeant, Detective Hardin, Jeannie and three other uniformed officers entered. They started with the front room and kitchen area.

"Remember what we're dealing with. Be super careful what you touch. I meant it when I said that shit is bad. Don't want to lose my FBI agent to frog sweat," Hardin said while laughing.

"Very funny. Is it a requirement for all Seattle's detectives to be jokesters?" Jeannie said while smiling.

"No, I was born with this unique ability, and working with the FBI just brings it out of me." While Hardin was saying this, he and Jeannie entered what appeared to be the assassin's computer room. Both of them gloved up, Jeannie opened the computer, but as suspected it was password protected.

"Not going to get anything from the computer here. Password protected. Do you want me to bag and tag it and send it to the bureau, or you guys want to handle it here?" Jeannie asked.

"As much as I'd like to say that we can handle it, because of the scrutiny this case will receive and already has, maybe the FBI can handle it better than we can. Please, be my guest."

"Well, thank you. Always nice to work collaboratively with other police agencies," Jeannie said jokingly.

"What do we have here?" said Hardin as he pulled out a safe deposit key from a drawer in the desk that held the computer. Jeannie smiled while looking at it in Hardin's hand.

"Do we know which bank or credit union?" she asked.

"Not yet," he replied. "But the morning is young. Patience dear grasshopper."

Jeannie smiling said, "Damn, you're really on a roll, aren't you?"

"Hardin," one of the uniform officers called from the kitchen area.

"Yeah, what do you have?"

The uniformed officer, also wearing latex gloves, met Hardin and Jeannie in the hallway, holding a plastic bottle about three inches tall labeled 2400 BBs. It looked like most of the BBs were still inside, but the discovery brought spontaneous smiles to Hardin, Jeannie, and the uniformed officer.

"I'm not sure what Ricin and frog poison looks like, but if you see anything, and I mean anything that looks suspicious, do not handle it. We'll get a hazmat team here. Got it? He stated to the officer.

"Loud and clear," was the response.

Returning to the computer room, Jeannie opened another desk drawer and found a receipt for a safe deposit box.

"Bingo," Jeannie said, slapping the receipt against her pants leg.

"Can it be that easy?" Hardin said.

Jeannie bagged the computer and told Hardin she would put a rush on it by carrying it with her on the plane back to the bureau. "That's one way to maintain the evidence chain," said Hardin and he secured the front door and placed Crime Scene tape on it. "Let's head to the bank and see if we luck out."

As expected, the bank would only verify that the key in their possession was for one of their safe deposit boxes. Any other information, including access to the box, would require a search warrant.

CHAPTER 38

Hardin called his office and requested that a detective call in for a telephonic search warrant, which would only take a few hours to secure. Hardin asked Jeannie is she was hungry and received a reply of "famished." He drove to an upscale hamburger joint and the two of them found a booth away from the other patrons. They placed their orders and initially exchanged small talk.

Jeannie decided to take this opportunity to bounce off some of her ideas about the recent slayings, including the Seattle murders, on Hardin. She pulled out a folded piece of paper containing her drawings from the night before. She turned the paper around to face Hardin and began outlining what the circles represented.

Hardin allowed Jeannie to explain the diagram without interruption, which she appreciated as it did not break her train of thought. She explained the secret Star Chamber court and how she felt that somehow it was the key. The easy part was explaining the various slayings Hardin was already aware of. Upon seeing the waitress bringing their food, Jeannie folded the paper and put it in her purse. When the waitress left, Hardin moved the condiments to the side of the table and asked Jeannie to put the diagram back.

"Here's what I see," Hardin said. "This is only a guess. I remember that old movie, *Star Chamber*. It was a great movie at the time: kind of like a death wish. It had a novel twist, with the killings orchestrated by a bunch of judges. Anyway, I agree with your assessment that all of these events emanate from the Star Chamber. Let's assume that there are a bunch of frustrated judges, just like the movie. They meet in secret and make judgments about people who aren't even aware they are being judged. I mean, look at the victims: they were all controversial, and from my political standpoint, all were left-wing liberals.

Look at the first individual, our former Secretary of State. What a corrupt bitch, but because of all her money and connections, she was above the law.

Next, we have Beaumont. If the rumors were correct, this asshole was funding all of these domestic terrorists' groups around the world to create his New World Order. Law enforcement agencies started to connect the dots with this scumbag, and what does he do when he feels the heat? He takes his prick of a son and anti-Jewish wife to some fucking mountain top in the Alps.

OK, who's next? Oh yeah, these two killings in downtown liberal Seattle," he said with disgust. "Don't get me started. Anyway, we have Blackstone. A cowardly little shit that organizes a bunch of snowflakes to violently protest any conservative gathering. And who's killed, sitting right next to him, that hippie, communist, gun smuggling cop killer, activist lawyer, Tillson. Do you see anything in common between all of these assholes?" Hardin asked while finally taking a bite of his burger.

"Shit, it was right there staring me in the face the whole time. All of these victims were all far-left loonies who used their power to incite or instigate various forms of anti-Americanism. As you said, Beaumont wanted open borders. A world-court. He advocated the elimination of national sovereignty. Funding people like Blackstone was a means to an end." She paused.

Hardin jumped back in saying, "As for the SDL, I think it's a group that gets their orders from the Star Chamber. The court meets, tries an individual, finds them guilty, and orders the SDL to carry out their sentence." He stopped giving Jeannie time to evaluate his assessment of her diagram.

Jeannie continued to munch on a fry after sliding it through some catsup, staring intently at the paper. She pointed to the circle containing the name Judge Baldwin. "You know, none of this would've come to light if we had not arrested this guy for child porn. His hidden files, of which we still have few more, mentioned this secret court and the SDL. From there, well, you get the idea. Everyone is somehow connected to the Star Chamber."

They finished lunch and took a quick tour of the Fish Market and CenturyLink Stadium, home of the Seattle Seahawks. Jeannie told Hardin she had been a big fan of the San Francisco 49ers until one of their former quarterbacks became an ass refusing to stand for the National Anthem. Not only that, but when she heard he was wearing socks of police depicted as pigs, that was the last straw for her. She had not watched an NFL game in years, she said.

Hardin's cellphone rang and after answering, told Jeannie the warrant was ready. They returned to his car and drove back to the bank. The assistant manager had already researched the owner of the safe deposit box and was waiting for their return. "This way officers," she said as she guided them to an area near the vault housing over 200 safe boxes. "This is all the information we have on Mr. Burgess," she said as she handed some paperwork to Hardin. She then inserted her key into the top slot of the box, while Hardin did the same to the other slot. She showed Hardin how to remove the box, and once it was, left them alone in the room.

The box was stuffed with print-outs, pictures, thumb drives and maps. Examining the photos, they saw shots of the exterior of the coffee shop and the café chairs outside the main building. There were also articles about the assassination of a Bulgarian where the killer used a modified umbrella.

"Got him," Hardin said.

"Yes we do," said Jeannie.

CHAPTER 39

Jeannie was at SeaTac at 5:30 in the morning. She stopped at a Cinnabon's booth and got a roll and a cup of decaf. She slept well the night before after she and Hardin had pretty much solved the Star Chamber and slayings puzzle. She had not checked in with Davenport. "Fuck him," she thought. She had Burgess's computer and secured it in her carryon. She called and reached Flores at the bureau.

"Hey Jeannie, when are you coming home?" he asked.

"Look Flo, you didn't get this phone call, OK?" Jeannie said.

Jeannie filled him in on what she learned from her Hardin assist in Seattle. She told him she needed to clear up one item and would then return, and instructed him to make sure Darcy and Burk continue to keep a lid on the Judge Baldwin case. If approached by the SAC, they were to just give the asshole a bare minimum.

"Where are you going?" Flores asked.

"Better you don't know," she said. "Let Davenport think I'm still in Seattle. See you guys soon. Oh, and tell Burk and Darcy I have another computer for them to work on when I get back."

While waiting to board her plane, Jeannie felt bad for not being around to meet with Davenport's secretary, Stephanie. She checked the contact list on her phone and placed a call to Stephanie's home, hoping to catch her before she left for the field office. Stephanie answered, but Jeannie could tell her call awakened her.

"Hi Jeannie, where are you?" she asked.

"Why? Did Davenport ask about my status?" Jeannie responded.

"No, not really. Actually, he asked me yesterday afternoon if I you had checked in, and I said no. As far as I know, he has left your team alone also. So, how did it go up in Seattle?" she asked.

"All I can tell you on the phone is that it's big with a capital 'B.' Hey, I called to apologize for not being there so we could meet. How's it going with that prick, Davenport?" Jeannie listened and offered a suggestion.

Delaware was hot and humid. She took an Uber to the Wilmington Police Department, and after displaying her badge and identification, she was directed to the office of Captain Ted Simmons. She introduced herself to Simmons and was about to again show her identification, but he waved her off and pointed to a chair across from him and asked, "What can I do for you, Agent Loomis?"

Jeannie asked if it was still possible to view the residence of the late former secretary.

"Yes, it is, but we've pretty much closed the matter as an accidental death. Can I ask what interest the FBI has in the incident?" Captain Simmons asked.

Jeannie formulated an answer she hoped would only contain enough information to gain access to the home. She informed Simmons of the case in Seattle which he knew about, and embellished a few things that sounded factual. He seemed satisfied and picked up his phone, asking a detective named Ashford to come to his office. Captain Simmons introduced Jeannie to Ashford and told him to take her to the McKenzie home, asking for a uniformed officer to join them.

On the drive to the former secretary's estate, Ashford, who seemed naturally curious, asked the reason for going to the mansion. Jeannie laid on him the same line she gave Simmons, and that seemed to satisfy Ashford. The residence was, as Jeannie envisioned, a high priced piece of real estate that only a few wealthy individuals could afford, unless you were a highly connected politician – in other words, corrupt. It always amazed Jeannie that when a Democrat politician was running for office, how they tried to compare themselves with the poor, lower-middle-class populace; but, once in office they somehow turned their $174,000 a year salary into that of an millionaire. Of course, McKenzie, even before she became the Secretary of State, was rumored along with her late husband to be involved in numerous shady dealings in everything from real estate to hedge fund involvement, to sham charities.

Ashford asked the uniformed office to remain outside the front door. He unlocked the door and they entered the residence. The home still had a lived-in feeling, with furniture and flower arrangements exactly the way they were on the morning the former secretary decided to take a header. The whole house was hot, so Jeannie assumed someone decided to turn the air conditioner off since no one was living in it.

They reached the top of the stairs where Ashford pointed to a portion of the rug that had lifted from the tack board. "The secretary's two bodyguards heard her fall, and after checking on McKenzie and calling 9-1-1, one of them went up the stairs and found one of her slippers where the rug had lifted. He didn't touch it, but instead went into her bedroom and the other rooms on that floor and found them all empty. He then returned to the secretary and the two of them waited for the ambulance. Paramedics declared her dead. Looks like she caught her slipper on the rug and down she went." He said.

"Huh," Jeannie said as she started to bend down to get a closer look at the carpet. "The secretary never called out before she fell?"

"What do you mean?" Ashford responded.

"Well, you would think that in that brief moment when the secretary knew she was about to fall, she would have yelled or at least made some distress sound. Instead, she just fell. Something is not right."

Jeannie then squatted down by the frayed carpet. Looking at it, you could see that the carpet had not lifted itself from the tack board, but that someone had used a sharp object to pull it away just enough so that someone could envision the secretary catching her slipper on it.

"I hate to tell you that I think there's a problem with the scenario you guys have formulated. If you look closely at the rug and tack board, you can see some gouging with a sharp instrument on the tack board, as if someone was trying to pull part of the rug free. See?" as she motioned to Ashford.

Ashford looked, but acted a little defensively. "Could be, but still, it might have worked its way free on its own," he said while still squatted next to Jeannie. She stood and walked into the secretary's bedroom.

"Was it as hot and humid on the 4th of July as it is today?" Jeannie asked.

"Hell, it's been this hot for the last few weeks. The entire northeast coast has been engulfed with a heat weather system that is supposed to break in two days."

"So, the secretary and the two bodyguards would have had the air conditioner on, correct?" Jeannie asked while walking around the room and bed.

"Yes," he replied, and while pointing to the bedroom windows continued, "Both of those windows were also open that night since the secretary liked the windows left open slightly for fresh air, according to the two bodyguards and later, her maid."

"Really," Jeannie said as she approached the windows. Today she found both windows closed and locked. "So, if these windows were opened normally at night, that means there was no alarm system covering the third-floor, correct?"

"Yes, but the alarm system was active on the bottom floor except when one of the bodyguards conducted a random grounds inspection. He would shut off the intruder alarm and deactivate the motion detectors outside. Once he stepped outside, the other bodyguard would reactivate the intruder system. If the perimeter was clear, he would knock on the front door and the interior guard would shut off the intruder alarm, allowing the bodyguard to enter and then reactivate the whole system.

There is no way a person could have entered the residence without one, or both of the bodyguards or alarm system detecting something." Ashford stated in a defensive manner, probably anticipating that Jeannie was starting to come up with an alternative scenario.

Jeannie opened one of the windows and looked out. The roof was not steep compared to some of the other Victorian homes in the area. Finding nothing, she moved to the second window and in like manner, opened it. She first noticed that a neighbor's home was not far away and overlooked the McKenzie estate. She turned her back to the window and put her butt on the window sill. Holding on to the sides of the window frame, she was able to view the brick fireplace located directly above the window.

"Do you or the uniformed officer have access to a pair of binoculars?" she asked.

A little confused with the request, he recovered and said he didn't, but would check with the other officer.

"You're in luck. He had a pair in his patrol car." He handed the binoculars to Jeannie who again took her position hanging out of the window. She examined the brick fireplace, but was disappointed she did not find what she had hoped for. She then looked higher at the roof ridge, and there it was. She was positive.

"Can you request that the fire department come to this residence?" Jeannie asked Ashford.

"What for?" he responded.

"I think you have a homicide, not an accidental fall," Jeannie said.

CHAPTER 40

U pon landing, Jeannie had the Uber driver take her directly to her office. When she arrived she found Flores at his desk. "Hey, you're back." he said. Was the trip to Seattle worth it?"

Jeannie did not answer. Instead she pulled Burgess's computer from her carryon and waved at Flores to follow her. They both walked to Darcy's office. When they entered, Darcy jumped up and said to Jeannie and Flores, "You are both just in time."

Darcy took her seat and began moving the computer's mouse. While she was setting up, Burk brought Jeannie and Flores up to date. "We finally got into all of the judge's files. First, let me say he was a sick bastard. If any of the contents of his child porn files gets leaked to his future inmates, he's a dead man. The good news is that we now know where the Star Chamber is located."

"What? Where? What else did you find?" Jeannie asked.

Neither Burk nor Darcy said anything; they just smiled at each other. Then Burk got up and pulled a portable whiteboard to the front of the room. He pulled back a large sheet of butcher paper revealing several pictures of a massive estate designed in what Jeannie thought was gothic style. Burk had printed an address and "Star Chamber" in brackets under one of the photos. Another photo was an aerial shot showing the extensive size of the estate.

"Last night," Darcy said, "Burk and I were able to crack the final two files on the computer. We think the Star Chamber is a secret court, and somehow they communicate with a group called Sons and Daughters of Liberty, or simply SDL." Concluding her statement, she looked at Burk. Both of them seemed ready to be praised for their efforts. They were not disappointed as Jeannie said, "Great job."

Jeannie handed Burgess's laptop to Darcy. "Before opening it, let me bring all of this up to speed since what I'm about to tell you is huge. It's imperative that we tie everything together so we can get a search warrant for the Star Chamber and take down some very influential individuals.

For the next several minutes, Jeannie told her team about Interpol and the arrest of not only Cartwright, but several congressmen and celebrities. Next, she told them about the two assassinations that took place in Seattle, the method the killer used, and how he got injured leaving the scene. She showed them copies of all of the information found in his safe deposit box, and then pointed to the computer she had given to Darcy. "We don't have much time to keep everything we have under wraps. I want to see what's in his computer, and then we can decide on the best way to proceed."

Darcy and Burk started to decrypt the files on Burgess's computer. Flores and Jeannie decided to let them do their thing, and walked back to Jeannie's office. "So, did the SAC leave you guys alone while as I was away, or was he snooping?" she asked.

"Never saw nor heard from the prick," Flores said.

"Good. I asked Agent Delaney at Interpol to try and hold the media off until we completely understand what we have here, but with those asshole congressmen, who knows how long he can realistically put them off." Her cellphone rang, and with dread she saw it was Davenport.

She showed the cellphone screen to Flores, and he gave the phone his middle finger. "Hello, this is Agent Loomis," Jeannie said, acting as if she did not know the ID of the caller.

"Loomis, I need to see you in my office, now." With that, he hung up.

"I've been summoned, and it sounds like an ass-chewing is waiting for me when I get there," she told Flores.

"Hey, tell him you're pregnant and maybe he'll go easy on you," Flores said.

"Screw you," Jeannie said with a smile on her face as she left the room.

CHAPTER 41

Before entering Davenport's office, she ran into Stephanie in the hallway. "Glad I found you before you went in," she said. "He's pissed. A Captain Simmons from the Wilmington Police Department called him. He was on the phone with him for less than five minutes and then, after hanging up, he came storming into my office asking, and I quote: "Where the fuck is she?"

I told him the last I'd heard, you were in Seattle. He yelled that you weren't in Seattle and to find you, but then changed his mind and said he'd track you down himself, so be prepared."

Jeannie thanked Stephanie and said she should probably go and either get some coffee or use the bathroom so that Davenport wouldn't by chance see them together before she entered his office.

"You sure?" Stephanie asked.

"Hey, what can he do, fire me for doing my job?" Jeannie said, not waiting for an answer as she continued down the hall to Davenport's office.

"Come in," shouted Davenport after Jeannie knocked on his door. Yup, Stephanie was right, he was pissed. "Take a seat", he said. "I just got off the phone with a Captain Simmons of the Wilmington Police Department. You want to tell me what the fuck you were doing in Delaware when I gave you a direct order to go to Seattle?"

In the short time she had after leaving Stephanie in the hall, Jeannie had decided how much she would tell Davenport until she and her team had all the information about the Star Chamber, SDL, the assassinations, Judge Baldwin, and Cartwright.

"Yes sir, I did as you ordered and flew to Seattle. I thought that my involvement with the Seattle Police Department would be to offer federal assistance if requested. Instead, it quickly became clear that Detective Sergeant Hardin and I were to follow up evidence in a rapidly developing series of events." Jeannie paused.

"I'm waiting," said Davenport.

"Well, the suspect was in a coma after being involved in a traffic accident while leaving the scene. After running his prints and getting a positive ID, Sergeant Hardin obtained a search warrant for his residence and later, for a safe deposit box.

"Yeah," Davenport said in an exasperated voice, "This is a great story, but how the hell did you end up in Delaware?"

"Well sir, I'm sure you're aware of the murders of Beaumont and his family, followed by the slayings in Seattle," she responded.

"Yes, I'm aware, go on," he said.

"Well, I thought that maybe there was a connection with the death of former Secretary of State McKinzie, and since the killer or killers of Beaumont are still unknown, I felt expedience was in order."

"Do you know how embarrassing it is for this agency, more specifically me, to receive a call from Captain Simmons thanking me for your involvement in their case and the embarrassment they avoided if they had gone forward and closed the case as an accidental death?" Not waiting for an answer, he said, "Your actions border on gross insubordination and I'm formally advising you that I will be recommending disciplinary action. After a review of my initial report by human resources, I believe you can expect formal suspension. For now, you'll continue your role with your team until further notice. You can leave."

Jeannie left his office just a little shocked about the insubordination charge. She expected an ass-chewing, but now the asshole wanted to go formal.

CHAPTER 42

"What happened?" Flores asked as Jeannie entered her office.

"The bastard is bringing me up on an insubordination charge. If human resources and the administration above Davenport agree, I will face suspension. Who knows, maybe the motherfucker will transfer my ass to North Dakota. Never mind, has Darcy and Burk had any success on Burgess's computer yet?

"Yeah, they just called your desk phone, and when I answered they said they'd found something and wanted to know where you were. Guess we should head down there," he said.

"Jeannie," Burk said as if out of breath.

"You guys broke into his files?" Jeannie asked.

"Not yet," he said, "But while Darcy and I were trying to get into his files, we found an encrypted email that was sent a day and a half ago. Using some of the same methods we used on Judge Baldwin's computer, we were able to get in and found the email labeled High Priority.

"You opened it?" Jeannie asked.

"Here it is," said Darcy, as she turned the computer so Jeannie and Flores could view it.

From SDL
Priority Target in 48 hours.
Target will be revealed at met with handler - 24 hours at normal place/time.
Assisted by two SDL members.
Text acknowledgment.

"Holy shit," said Flores as everyone in the room looked at Jeannie. "What time did the email arrive?" he asked.

"Let's see," said Darcy as she turned the computer back to herself. "It came in at 8:32 p.m.."

Everyone looked at a timing device, with Burk the first to calculate that there were less than twelve hours left before a target or targets were going to get hit.

CHAPTER 43

The flight from Switzerland arrived at 9:15 a.m. She had no carryon, opting to pack a suitcase so she could bring back some souvenirs from California. Liberal ass California, where she would not be harassed for looking transgender. This was a first for her, teaming up with other members of the SDL. Should be interesting as long as he or she doesn't get in my way, she thought. It was also the first time she had ever visited California. She was not impressed when the Uber driver took her to her hotel in downtown Sacramento.

The second killer decided after receiving a priority email that it would be quicker to fly from Southern California than to drive. He had to make sure he arrived ahead of the meet so he could get a room, and upon learning of its location, check it out. An Asian male in his early twenties, he got off the plane at the Sacramento International Airport wearing an LA Dodgers hat backward, a jean jacket and dark pants. He used his app to call for a Lyft driver and told him the name of his motel. No reason to blow a lot of money since he would be leaving the day after the hit.

The third SDL member was already in Sacramento. Born and raised there, he could not wait to move to Idaho or Montana and get away from the bleeding-heart liberals that had destroyed his state. "Shit," he said to himself, our last governor was all for allowing perverts to use the same bathroom as children. And one of the cities, can't remember which one, banned straws but allow open drug use, even providing needles."

That night, each received a priority text telling them the location of the meet: The California Railroad Museum located near Old Sacramento. The text said to be there promptly at 9 a.m. The SDL member who lived in Sacramento knew the area well. Good spot he thought: lots of tourists, a lot of people in groups. He did not need to scout the area ahead of time.

She had no idea where the train museum was, nor what to expect. Talking to a woman at the front desk of her hotel, she learned that the museum was within walking distance and decided to walk. She enjoyed viewing the shops in Old Town Sacramento and bought an ice cream and some red-colored popcorn. Finding the museum, she casually walked around the perimeter to familiarize herself with the surroundings should anything happen that would necessitate an escape.

She saw the Asian male standing across the street from the museum checking her out. He had to be a member of the SDL casing the area, she thought.

Nine a.m. arrived. The three converged at the museum, focusing on each other as well as a middle-aged Black male acting as if he were taking pictures. While still in the act of taking photos and without looking at the three individuals, he reached into a large stuffed backpack and pulled out three identical 8 ½" by 11" photos. While each of them stared at the photo, again with his back turned away from them, he said, "This is your target. It's a satellite office of the FBI in Roseville."

"Where is Roseville?" the Asian male asked.

"It's not far from here: maybe 20-30 minutes," the Sacramento native said.

"The target's an FBI building? Are you kidding me?" asked the female.

"It's a minimally staffed satellite office. By 4p.m., which is the time we want you to act, at most, there will be five agents inside." He reached into the backpack again and gave each of them another photo. "Your target is not a person. We want you to locate this computer and all documents you can find related to Star Chamber. This photo shows you the layout of the building. Of course, if you meet resistance, you'll take them out. Once you've secured the computer and related material, head back to your room and wait for a follow up text naming our next meet. I suggest the three of you grab something to eat together and discuss your plans. Time is of the essence."

He gave each person a small duffle bag from the backpack. As each of them grabbed it, they presumed it contained a weapon due to its size, shape and weight.

CHAPTER 44

Jeannie contemplated informing the SAC, but what did she and her team have that could be acted upon? No known location. The only time element was that whatever was going to happen, would take place in less than two hours. No, instead she and her team had to continue and try to discover what else was on Burgess's computer.

She sent Flores out to pick up hamburgers, fries, and sodas for her and her team. Stephanie came by to say goodnight and to warn Jeannie that the SAC was still in his office. Jeannie said goodnight as did the rest of her team, and Stephanie left.

Burk and Darcy pressed on while Jeannie returned to her office and started the long task of typing her report which would encompass everything, starting with the files on Judge Baldwin's computer and his involvement with Cartwright. Every so often she looked at the wall-mounted clock and took note of the passing time.

At 4p.m. she heard footsteps coming down the hallway from Davenport's office. "Here comes the asshole," she told herself. She closed the file she was working on and brought up another one dealing with an older bank robbery case she had to provide testimony the following week. Knowing Davenport, the jerk would probably maneuver around her back so he could gaze on her computer screen to see what she was doing. That was one of the things that Stephanie said he liked to do while getting a look at her boobs. "What a pervert," she thought.

Sure enough, Davenport walked directly into Jeannie's office. He started to walk around behind her; but she stood, acting as if he had startled her. That caused him to stop his advance. Before he said anything, there was a loud bang and the breaking of glass. Jeannie saw a smoke canister spin across the hallway that Davenport had just exited. Before Davenport could react, a female suspect quickly spun around the corner and shot him one time. A headshot sprayed blood on the wall behind him. Jeannie, partially blocked by Davenport's falling body, fell behind her desk while pulling out her weapon. She quickly got a shot off at the female who had to wait until Davenport hit the ground to get a better angle on Jeannie.

While Jeannie was exchanging shots with the female, she saw two other individuals dressed in black run down the hallway to where Burk and Darcy were located. She heard more shots while the hallway and Jeannie's office filled with gun smoke.

The two individuals who had run down the hallway were now retreating. One of them shouted to the female, "Got it, let's go."

The female shouted at Jeannie, calling her a bitch, and with a new clip fired several more times while retreating. Jeannie was hit in the stomach as well as her left shoulder. She tried to get up, but the pain in her abdomen was too intense. She placed her hand on Davenport's carotid artery, but he was gone. His eyes were open, appearing to focus on the clock on the wall.

Flores returned from his burger run and saw a crowd beginning to form outside the main access door. He yelled at them to move as he pulled out his weapon. He saw the shattered glass door. Shouting, "FBI," he entered the building, calling out to Jeannie, who answered him by saying, "I'm hit! Possible active shooters inside," she said.

Flores dialed 9-1-1 and rushed to Jeannie's side. "Jesus, what happened?" He then focused on the SAC.

"He's gone. Go check on Darcy and Burk," she said.

Again, announcing, " FBI," Flores slowly made his way down the hallway to Darcy's office. He saw Burk laying on his side with blood emanating from his wound. "Hang in there, buddy," he said to Burk who was semi-conscious. "Where's Darcy?"

Burk told him that Darcy had gone to the restroom when the two gunmen came in. Just then, Darcy ran to her office and kneeled by Burk, tears rolled down her cheeks. "Are you alright?" Flores asked her.

"Yes, has anyone called 911?' she asked.

"Yes, I dialed. They're on their way," he responded.

"You stay with Burk. I have to check on Jeannie. She was hit also." With that, he left Darcy and went to Jeannie's office and found her unconscious.

CHAPTER 45

Roseville Police officers, fire fighters and paramedics began filling the FBI satellite office. Other FBI agents soon arrived and set up a command center. Jeannie and Burk were immediately placed on gurneys after receiving triage. They had to be transported in separate ambulances since both required intensive care by the paramedic in each vehicle.

After giving a quick statement, Flores headed to the hospital where Jeannie and Burk had been taken. Upon arrival, Flores was informed that both had already been taken to surgery. Flores felt it necessary to tell the nurse that Jeannie was probably pregnant. She said she would inform the doctor and told him where the waiting room was located.

About forty-five minutes later, Darcy showed up at the waiting room. "How are they?" she asked.

"Don't know. When I got here the nurse told me they had both been taken into surgery."

"My God. We were the target," Darcy said.

"No, I don't think so," Flores said while shaking his head. "I mean, think about it. Yes, Davenport was a complete jerk and a certified asshole, but why would a team of three killers storm an FBI satellite office and take him out? You can say the same thing about Jeannie, Burk, you, me. None of us warrant being assassinated. No, they were after something else," Flores said.

"What exactly do you remember?" Flores asked.

"We were working on a particular file that Burgess had on his computer. He was very paranoid about his involvement with the Star Chamber and SDL, and decided to do his investigation by following one of his contacts after a meet," she said.

"Jesus, did he list names, locations, anything we could use?" Flores said.

"Before I went to the bathroom, we found the address of the Star Chamber, similar to what we got off Judge Baldwin's laptop. He had another file we hadn't opened yet labeled 'Judges of the Star Chamber.' I left Burk working on it." She started to cry and reached out for Flores. "While I was in the bathroom, I heard a loud bang and breaking glass, followed by gunshots. I didn't have my weapon, so I hid in the bathroom. Oh my God, I hope they make it."

"Shit, I know what they wanted," said an excited Flores. "They were after Judge Baldwin's computer. The Star Chamber wanted to get the computer since they don't know what's on it. I need to get back to the office and check with forensics to see if the computer is still there," Flores said as he started towards the exit doors.

"Wait," Darcy said. I think you're right. Check to see if Burgess's computer is there also," Darcy said as Flores left the hospital. Other agents began arriving.

Burk's elderly mother arrived at the hospital, driven by her neighbor. Darcy had met her in the past and hugged once she recognized her. "How is my son?" she asked. Darcy, wiping a few tears from her eyes, filled her in with what she knew, which hadn't changed since she arrived at the hospital.

The first update came regarding Burk. The female surgeon said he was stabilized and would recover from a gunshot wound that collapsed one lung and broke two ribs. "He'll be sore for a little while, but he'll be fine," she told a grateful mother. She had no information about Jeannie.

Flores returned and asked it forensics was through in Darcy's office. He was cleared to enter. Inside, as he suspected, not only was Judge Baldwin's computer gone, but so was Burgess's computer . All the documents that had been spread out on the two tables about the Star Chamber investigation, SDL, and Cartwright were gone. It looked like the shooters took whatever documents they could find along with the computers. That was the target. Davenport, Jeannie, and Burk were just collateral damage.

CHAPTER 46

Flores returned to the hospital and told Darcy that everything had been taken from her office. Even in haste, the killers had been meticulous in what they had stolen. "I put two backup thumb drives on the desk. Did you see them?" she asked.

Flores, shaking his head said that everything was gone from the top of her desk. "Do you know if Burk kept anything?" he asked.

"Not that I know of. Since we were working together, I never thought someone would be brazen enough to assault an FBI building," she responded.

"Yeah, I've been thinking about that. How did they get the information about the layout of the building, and the number of agents inside? Someone from the inside leaked the information, and if I find them, they will not have a day in court."

Before Darcy could respond, a male surgeon came out and asked if any of Jeannie's relaltives were present. Flores lied and said he was her brother--instead of the usual run around about only giving medical information to loved ones. Flores walked with the surgeon away from Darcy to be confidential. The surgeon did not question Flores's relationship and proceeded to tell him that Jeannie was still in critical shape but should make it. They recovered two bullets, one from her shoulder and one from her abdomen. As expected, the abdomen wound was the most serious. He had to remove a section of her stomach, but baring an infection, she should survive. Then he remorsefully added that she had lost the fetus.

Flores did not act surprised about the loss of the fetus, long suspecting that Jeannie was pregnant. He wondered, however, if she ever checked to confirm the possibility.

"When can I see her," Flores asked the departing surgeon.

"She'll remain sedated until at least late tomorrow morning, and even then I will restrict the amount of visitor time. But, if I were you, I would go home and get some sleep. There's nothing you can do for her now."

Flores told Darcy what the doctor said. He gave Darcy the same advice he got from the surgeon about going home and getting some rest. He said that he would be back at the hospital at 7 a.m. to see how Jeannie did during the night, and asked Darcy to stop at the office tomorrow morning to take inventory of what had been taken. "Get ready for a lot of administrator types flying in from Washington to evaluate what happened and put their two cents in. Just answer their questions as honestly as you can. Don't let them intimidate you," Flores said.

Running a little late due to traffic, Flores arrived at the hospital at 7:20 a.m. He was told by a nurse that Jeannie was still asleep, but that they would awaken her at 7:30 and take her vitals. He decided to check in on Burk. Burk was sitting up and had a ventilation tube in his left nostril. He seemed alert and gave a thumbs up to Flores when he saw him at the door.

"I heard about people doing anything they can to get some extra vacation time? How do you feel man? You look like shit," Flores said.

Burk raised his right hand since his left hand had two IV's inserted, and twisted it up and down indicating that he was so-so. His mother entered the room and said hi to Flores. She then went to the table next to her son's bed and gave him a small 8" by 10" whiteboard and marker.

"He can't talk very well with that tube up his nose. I picked this up at the gift shop and he seems to like it." She bent down and kissed him on his forehead. "Well, I'll leave you two alone so you can talk. I'm going down to the cafeteria and get some breakfast. If I don't eat, I start getting headaches. Price of getting old, I guess."

Burk, using the whiteboard asked how Jeannie was?

Flores said that she was going to make it, that she had been shot twice, once in the shoulder, and once in the stomach.

Burk wrote "ouch" on the whiteboard.

Burk asked if there were any leads on the shooters, with Flores stating not yet. He told Burk about both computers being taken and all the related documents missing. He then asked Burk if he had created separate files or other documents that the killers may have overlooked. Burk wrote "No."

Flores left, telling Burk he would see him later that afternoon and give him any update information that may have turned up during the day. He tapped the Burk's right foot and left.

CHAPTER 47

H e found Jeannie barely awake when he got to her room. She was wearing an oxygen mask and slowly removed it, showing a smile and uttering "Hi."

"Gee, must be the hospital food since you look just as bad as old Burk," he said chuckling. She smiled but wasn't alert enough to give him a comeback. Softly, she asked Flores how Burk was, and Flores gave her the latest prognosis. He told her that Burk's mother was at his side, and that he was using a whiteboard to communicate because of the nasogastric tube.

"You heard I lost the baby?" she asked.

Flores wasn't sure how to respond; he just dropped his head and gave it an affirmative nod.

"Maybe just as well. I would probably have been a terrible mother," she said.

"Hey, don't say that. If you are half as good a mother as you are a team leader, then your future kids are going to be great," Flores said, trying desperately to come up with a witticism. He pulled up a chair told Jeannie what had happened after she got shot. He included a recent phone call he got from Darcy that morning-- that both computers and all related documents had been taken off the two desks. Jeannie did not interrupt him, but did ask questions when he was through.

"Any idea who the killers were? How did they know the layout of the office? How did they know we'd be the only ones inside? Has anyone got a search warrant for the Star Chamber?" Pretty much the same questions Flores and Darcy discussed last night.

Flores told her his suspicions, and that he and Darcy were going to be debriefed at 1 p.m. He planned on bringing this up. He also told her that an acting SAC arrived this morning from the Sacramento office, and he had already given him all the information they had to date.

"I think you'll like the new SAC. He's very professional. Seems old school. He had an agent from the Sacramento office write everything down, and they're probably seeking a search warrant right now for the Star Chamber," as he looked at his watch. "I told him to notify me so I can go along for the search," Flores said.

Just then a young lady dressed in scrubs entered the room with a large bouquet. "Hi," she said. "These are for you." She placed the vase on a counter and handed Jeannie a card.

Jeannie looked at Flores and said, "You didn't have to do this."

"It wasn't me. I would have snuck in Big Mac or something," Flores jokingly replied.

"It's from Stephanie. How nice. How is she doing?" Jeannie asked Flores.

"Knee-deep with brass, both from our branch office in Sacramento: but, also a lot of big wigs from Washington. She told me she felt a little guilty about Davenport getting killed. I asked her why and she told me she had filed a formal sexual harassment complaint against him along with another about him maintaining a hostile work environment. Doesn't matter now huh?" he asked, not expecting an answer.

Flores and Darcy endured a long debriefing with Darcy's taking the longest. Flores could only provide information about the team's effort in the Cartwright, Judge Baldwin, and related matters since he was out of the office during the time of the assault. After his questioning, he told them of his deep concern about how the killers received their information to pull off such a precise attack.

Darcy was drilled on why none of the information had been backed up. She later told both Flores, Burk, and Jeannie that everyone on the team was working as fast as they could to identify those responsible for the killings, and to figure out who the next target might be. She said it seemed to satisfy most of the senior personnel's questions, except for some computer geek that said he would have immediately backed up everything. Those around this guy started rolling their eyes when he opened his mouth.

CHAPTER 48

The three met again with their handler at the railroad museum. As before he posing as a photographer taking pictures of the museum and its surroundings. All three killers arrived at the same time, with the Asian male and female carrying backpacks.

"I trust that in these backpacks I will find a computer, documents, and weapons?" he asked.

None of the three initially answered; but, while the two with the backpacks handed them to him, the second male said there were two laptops in addition to all the paperwork they could seize.

"Excellent. Job well done," the handler said as he put the two backpacks down by his leg. "I must inform you that our apparatus will temporarily be down until we see how things shape up after your raid. Your fees will be deposited into your accounts by 5 p.m. this evening. Thank you. You are all true patriots."

The three took this statement as being dismissed and departed without saying anything to each other. One had an early flight to Los Angeles, while the other decided to spend at least a day checking out San Francisco before flying back to Switzerland. The third hailed an Uber and was well on his way back to his residence.

The gavel struck the base the night before the planned assault on the FBI satellite office.

"Gentlemen, please take your seat," Judge Silverman said, using the microphone in front of him due to a sore throat, and called the Star Chamber to order.

"Thank all of you for attending this emergency session of the Star Chamber. Per my one-on-one phone call with each of you, we hope by this time tomorrow, to have in our possession, possible damaging information that Judge Baldwin kept on his computer in direct violation of our bylaws. That said, I believe it would be prudent that we temporarily suspend future sessions of this body until the cooling-off period passes. During the interim, you shall continue to select individuals you feel need to be reviewed by this tribunal in the future. In addition, I believe it is prudent that we have the SDL eliminate those involved in the retrieval of the damaging information Judge Baldwin had on his computer. I will now call the roll to see if we are all in agreement. Please signify with "aye" or "nay" if you support the motion.

"Judge Roberts?"

"Aye."

"Judge Swartz?"

"Aye."

"Judge Kalford?"

"Aye."
"Judge Hall?"
"Aye."
"Judge Henderson?"
"Aye."
"Judge Kavanaugh?"
"Aye."
"Judge Kanamoto?"
"Aye."
"Very well, I cast my aye vote making it a unanimous decision. Until further notice the Star Chamber is dark." Judge Silverman struck the gavel against the base and the judges began to depart.

Within ten minutes after the last car left the Star Chamber, four vans arrived. A total of twenty individuals got out of the vans dressed in white custodian overalls. They began taking out a large garbage can and cleaning solvent. Three and a half hours later, they left.

CHAPTER 49

T hirteen days later and after a few setbacks, Jeannie was being pushed in a wheelchair by a male intern to the exit doors of the hospital. Burk had beaten her by six days. Flores, Darcy, as well as Stephanie, added to her escort. The sun felt good on her face once she got outside. Flores had left the group and ran to get his vehicle. Pulling it into the patient pick up zone, the male intern helped Jeannie get into the front seat. She got a hug from everyone except Flores who was still seated in the driver's seat.

"OK, enough of this Hallmark stuff. Let me get this lady home." Flores said as he started the car. Returning good-by waves, Jeannie looked at the hospital and realized how lucky she was, except for losing her baby which caused her to start crying.

As Jeannie was being discharged from the hospital, a small army of federal agents in black Suburban SUVs advanced onto the estate where the Star Chamber was located. Heavily armed, they found the front and rear doors unlocked. The agents that entered immediately smelled the odor of commercial cleaning material. For some it equated with the smell of chlorine bleach; for others it smelled of the outdoors after a thunderstorm: in another word, clean.

Their search found no trace of anyone having been in the large auditorium they assumed was used as the court chamber. Bathrooms did not reveal any prints nor DNA. The place had been scrubbed thoroughly. FBI paper chasers became frustrated when their investigation of building ownership became snarled in Shell Corporation after Shell Corporation. From Tokyo, Japan, to Kiev, Ukraine, and from Bangladesh to all other major cities and countries, they failed to track down anyone to interrogate about the Star Chamber.

While still recuperating at home, Jeannie had been similarly interviewed by her superiors as were Burk, Darcy, and Flores. The questions posed to her did not seem career-threatening; but perhaps, she thought, they were slow-balled her due to her weakened condition. Even though she had heard through the grapevine that nothing was found at the Star Chamber location, her superiors filled her in on the status of the case.

After they left, she thought about the similarities between this case and the Ark investigation. Shit, in the Ark investigation, the end result was nothing. But in this case, her team had exposed a sex-trafficking ring involving children. They caught the mastermind behind the trafficking and child pornography, and his infamous sex island. A pervert judge and a significant number of congressmen, sports celebrities, and Hollywood A-listers took a major hit to their respective careers, and the Deep State had no power to help them. "Love it," she thought.

But, like the Ark investigation, Jeannie still had a lot of unanswered questions. Who were the judges that held secret proceedings in the Star Chamber? What was the identity of the killers responsible for the murders of McKenzie, Beaumont--his son and wife, Blackstone, and Tillson? Who shot her and Burk? What is the makeup of the SDL--this Sons and Daughters of Liberty group? How did all of this get started? Who financed the whole operation? Will it start up again? And, even more importantly, who provided the information leading to the attack on the FBI office?

CHAPTER 50

On his way back to his home in Sacramento, he stopped at a gas station and changed his clothes, putting those he wore during the shootout into a dumpster. He was now day-dreaming about what he wanted to buy with the money he earned from the FBI assault. "Man, that was intense," he thought.

For $25,000 he could purchase a vintage 1963 Fender Stratocaster electric guitar he was watching on eBay. It would sure be an upgrade from the guitar he was using now with his band.

"But," he thought, "Twenty-five grand would be a nice down payment on a new 2020 mid-engine Corvette." He would still owe over forty-thousand even with that big of a down payment, but what a hell of a machine.

He checked his freezer and pulled out a frozen pizza and pre-heated his oven. He turned on his air condition and changed into his swim trunks. He might as well get in a swim before he puts the pizza in the oven. Opening the sliding glass door, the pool awaited. He walked around to the deep end but remembered he forgot a towel. After returning from the house, he placed it on a patio chair and again made his way to the deep end of the pool.

All the symptoms occurred at once: muscle spasms, breathing problems, seizures, and loss of consciousness. He trashed about for only a few seconds, if that. The electric shock emanating from the underwater pool light easily generated enough watts to take his life. He would not be found until later that evening when a neighbor, peering over the fence, would see his lifeless body floating on the surface.

She spent several days in San Francisco sightseeing and buying souvenirs for her friends back home. The lifestyle she saw on display in the downtown area of the city excited her. No one seemed to have any inhibitions. She liked that, although seeing people relieve themselves in front of her on the street seemed "sick," not to mention the number of hypodermic needles lying all over the sidewalks. She boarded her plane back to Stockholm, and after an uneventful flight made it safely home where she slept off and on for two days. Probably from the adrenaline rush, she thought.

On Saturday night she was mentally ready to party. She dressed up in her favorite leather outfit, including a large dog collar around her neck, and headed to her favorite bar. The place was packed. She could hear and feel the pulsing music a block away. "Going to be a good night," she thought.

The female that approached her was interesting, also dressed in leather and sporting a spiked hairdo. They seemed to hit it off instantly. Dancing and matching shots of Tequila, she forgot about her shootout with the FBI only a few days earlier. At 2:30a.m., she decided to invite her new "friend" back to her apartment. Her friend asked her to stop at a liquor store first so they could continue their buzz, so she did.

Back at her place, she took out two glasses and poured more shots. She had to pee and excused herself, but before she headed to the bathroom, she leaned into her new friend and French kissed. "I liked that," she said as she hurried off.

When she returned, she was only wearing her panties and bra. Her friend handed her another shot while returning her a kiss. After the kiss, they both downed the shot and refilled their glasses. They held their glasses in one hand while exploring each other's breasts, first outside and then inside their bras.

God, she thought, now is not the time to become sleepy, but she could not stop herself from wanting to lay down and drift off to dreamland. She became dizzy. Her friend was so nice. She even helped her get into bed. She was out cold and did not feel the syringe containing an arsenic compound flood her carotid artery.

The Asian, riding his BMW 1200S bike, capable of going from zero to sixty in just 3.2 seconds, shot through the curves of Mulholland Drive, reaching speeds in excessive of 100 mph. He cursed having to wear a helmet—as if that were going to do him a lot of good at this speed, he thought. At three in the morning, there was very little traffic impeding his venture. He knew Dead Man's Curve was coming up and each time he approached this deadly section of the road, he always applied a little more speed.

He saw a van parked to the side of the road as he was racing to Dead Man's Curve. Going so fast, he never saw the van's side door open, nor the individual holding some type of device in his hands. What he did see was his front tire explode of as he entered the curve. Having no time to react, he went sailing over the side of the roadway down the sides of the canyon walls. The first of many impacts killed him.

CHAPTER 51

When Jeannie returned to work she found her office filled with flowers, balloons, and a huge box of chocolates on her desk. She was surprised when there was a knock on her door and upon opening it, her whole team--Darcy, Stephanie, and the new SAC--entered with Stephanie carrying a decorated cake escribed with WELCOME BACK JEANNIE!

Jeannie started to cry, and almost on cue Flores said, "Here we go with the Hallmark thing."

Everyone laughed, and as Jeannie wiped her eyes with a tissue, she was introduced to the new SAC by Stephanie. Her new superior told her he wanted her to go home early each day that week, and that was an order.

No more information came in about the Star Chamber. The paper chasers had given up. The media whom Jeannie thought were part of the Deep State, were not able to generate any sympathy for those caught in the sex investigation, since it was conducted by Interpol. Judge Baldwin had escaped the sweep by Interpol, but Jeannie and her team would await his arrival the following morning when he would be taken into custody upon landing on U.S. soil.

Jeannie returned a call she had received from Agent Delaney that expressed his gratitude for her and her team's help in arresting those on "sex" island. He shared the names of celebrities arrested, and none came as a surprise to her. He also wanted to make sure she was OK, and the two agreed to have lunch together in the future.

The next morning Judge Baldwin was taken into custody by Jeannie and Flores after he had located his luggage and was heading for an airport exit. Belligerent, and threatening both of them with the loss of their federal jobs, he refused to cooperate and was booked into a federal correctional facility. They would deal with him later after he got a taste of incarceration.

On her second day on the job, Stephanie called Jeannie telling her that the SAC would like to see her when convenient. Davenport never was so considerate, but she thought to herself that God should have mercy on his soul.

Stephanie hugged her upon entering the outer office to the SAC. "How do you feel," she asked.

"Fine. I get a little sleepy after lunch, but then I go home and take a power nap, and then I feel fine. The doctor said I can return to eating what I want, so that is nice."

"He's waiting for you. Let me knock," Stephanie said.

When Jeannie entered she was surprised to see not only the acting SAC, but the Deputy Director who had flown in from Washington D.C. "Damn! Stephanie could have given me a heads-up," she thought.

"Good morning Jeannie. How do you feel?" asked the SAC, motioning for her to take a seat.

"Fine sir," she responded.

"I assume you recognize Deputy Director Bill Thompson who flew in late last night to be here this morning," the SAC stated.

Before Jeannie could answer, the deputy director leaned forward in his seat and offered his hand. They both shook hands and the deputy director also asked how her recuperation was going.

After pleasantries were exchanged, the SAC looked at the deputy director as if to say the floor was his. The deputy director commended Jeannie and the work she and her team had done on what was a massive international investigation. What he told her next was to remain in the office between the three of them. Jeannie said she understood, and the deputy director rose before speaking.

"Agent Loomis," the deputy director said, speaking formally now, "this evening the President will announce that the Director of the FBI will be resigning. I won't get into the particulars surrounding his resignation, but let's just say 'politics,' shall we? I will be acting as the interim director with no desire to assume the position full time, hoping that the President can find someone to permanently fill the job as soon as possible. I like being just where I am. But I will tell you that the new appointee, whoever it will be, will be given a mandate from the new attorney general to clean house." He paused giving Jeannie time to process the information.

"With that in mind, early this morning the SAC and I interviewed your team members. They were all highly complementary about your abilities as a team leader. That made our job a lot easier. At this time Agent Loomis, we want to offer you the post of SAC.

ABOUT THE AUTHOR

Amazon best-selling author of *Hitting Rock Bottom,* Dr. Gary Rose returns with another riveting thriller involving FBI agent Jeannie Loomis first introduced in *Ark of the Covenant – Raid on the Church of Our Lady Mary of Zion.* Investigating what appeared to be an unrelated child pornography case, Loomis and her team begin to connect the dots of killings targeting societies elite who seemed to be above the law.

Living in the foothills of Northern California, and teaching at-risk incarcerated adults, Dr. Rose continues to be inspired by family and friends who provide new situations for Agent Loomis.

CPSIA information can be obtained
at www.ICGtesting.com
Printed in the USA
BVHW031415311019
562603BV00004B/30/P